A Partisan's Daughter

ALSO BY LOUIS DE BERNIÈRES

The War of Don Emmanuel's Nether Parts

Señor Vivo and the Coca Lord

The Troublesome Offspring of Cardinal Guzman

Captain Corelli's Mandolin

Sunday Morning at the Centre of the World

Red Dog

Birds Without Wings

Louis de Bernières

A Partisan's Daughter

Harvill *Secker*
LONDON

Published by HARVILL SECKER 2008

2 4 6 8 10 9 7 5 3 1

First published in Great Britain in 2008 by
HARVILL SECKER
Random House, 20 Vauxhall Bridge Road,
London SW1V 2SA

www.rbooks.co.uk

Addresses for companies within The Random House Group Limited can be found at:
www.randomhouse.co.uk/offices.htm

The Random House Group Limited Reg. No. 954009

A CIP catalogue record for this book
is available from the British Library

ISBN 9781846552939

The Random House Group Limited supports The Forest Stewardship Council (FSC), the leading international forest certification organisation. All our titles that are printed on Greenpeace approved FSC certified paper carry the FSC logo. Our paper procurement policy can be found at www.rbooks.co.uk/environment

Mixed Sources
Product group from well-managed forests and other controlled sources
FSC
www.fsc.org Cert no. TT-COC-2139
© 1996 Forest Stewardship Council

Typeset in Bembo by Palimpsest Book Production Limited,
Grangemouth, Stirlingshire
Printed and bound in the UK by
CPI Mackays, Chatham ME5 8TD

'Le mariage bourgeois a mis notre pays en pantoufles, et bientôt aux portes de la mort.'

Albert Camus, *La Chute*

Contents

I

The Girl on the Street Corner

I am not the sort of man who goes to prostitutes.

Well, I suppose that every man would say that. People would disbelieve it just because you felt you had to say it. It's a self-defeating statement. If I had any sense I'd delete it and start again, but I'm thinking, 'My wife's dead, my daughter's in New Zealand, I'm in bad health, and I'm past caring, and who's paying any attention? And in any case, it's true.'

I did know someone who admitted it, though. He was a Dutchman who'd done it with a prostitute during his national service. He was in Amsterdam and he was suffering from blue balls at a time when he was on leave and had a little money in his pocket. He said she was a real stunner, and the sex was better than he had expected. However, the woman kept a bin by her bedside, the kind that is like a miniature dustbin, with a lid. You can still get them in novelty shops. Anyway, after he'd finished he eased off the condom, and she reached out and lifted the lid off for him out of good manners. It was packed to the brim with used condoms, like a great cake of pink and brown rubber. He was so horrified by that bin of limp milky condoms that he never went to a prostitute again. Mind you, I haven't seen him for twenty years, so he may well have succumbed by now. He liked to tell that story because he was an artist, and probably felt he had a Bohemian duty to be a little bit outrageous. I expect he was hoping I'd be shocked, because I am only a suburbanite.

I tried to go with a prostitute just once in my life, and it didn't work out as I had expected. It wasn't a case of blue balls so much as a case of loneliness. It was an impulse, I suppose. My wife was alive back then, but the trouble is that sooner or later, at best, your wife turns into your sister. At worst she becomes your enemy, and sets herself up as the principal obstacle to your happiness. Mine had obtained everything she wanted, so she couldn't see any reason to bother with me any more. All the delights with which she had drawn me in were progressively withdrawn, until there was nothing left for me but responsibilities and a life sentence. I don't think that most women understand the nature of a man's sexual drive. They don't realise that for a man it isn't just something quite nice that's occasionally optional, like flower arranging. I tried talking to my wife about it several times, but she always reacted with impatience or blank incomprehension, as if I was an importunate alien freshly arrived from a parallel universe. I never could decide whether she was being heartless or stupid, or just plain cynical. It didn't make any difference. You could just see her thinking to herself, 'This isn't my problem.' She was one of those insipid Englishwomen with skimmed milk in her veins, and she was perfectly content to be like that. When we married I had no idea that she would turn out to have all the passion and fire of a codfish, because she took the trouble to put on a good show until she thought it was safe not to have to bother any more. Then she settled in perpetuity in front of the television, knitting overtight stripy jumpers. She became more and more ashen-faced and inert. She reminded me of a great loaf of white bread, plumped down on the sofa in its cellophane wrapping. Englishmen don't like to talk about their troubles, but I've had enough conversations with other men like me, usually at a bar somewhere, usually trying to delay their homecoming, and always reading between the lines, to know how many of us get clamped into that claustrophobic dreary celibacy that stifles the flame inside them. They get angry and lonely and melancholy, and that's when the impulses come upon them. I sometimes wonder whether the reason that puritanical religious types are so keen on marriage is their certain knowledge that it's the one way to make sure that people get the least possible amount of sex.

The woman was standing on a street corner in Archway, looking as though she was pretending to wait for someone. She was wearing a short skirt and high boots, and her face was made up too much. I remember lilac lipstick, but I may have invented that image subsequently. It was winter, not that you'd ever know what season it was in Archway, because in Archway it's always late November on a good day, and early February on a bad one.

In fact it was during the Winter of Discontent. The streets were heaped high with rubbish, you couldn't buy bread or the *Sunday Times*, and in Liverpool no one would bury the dead. You couldn't get heating oil, and even if you had cancer you were lucky to get into hospital. The comrades in the trade unions were trying to start the revolution, and our particularly hopeless Prime Minister's ship was holed beneath the water. I've always liked being British, but that was the worst time I can remember, and the one time when it was impossible not to be depressed about living in Britain. Back then we all needed some prospect of consolation, even if you weren't married to a Great White Loaf.

The girl wore a fluffy white fur jacket. She had litter whirling about her in the cold wind, and she was like a light glowing in the fog. She seemed a well-built girl, and I felt a lurch of attraction that I couldn't help. There was a buzzing in my groin and a slightly sick feeling in my stomach.

It was the first time I'd ever knowingly spotted a prostitute, and I realised that I should just drive on. What if you get taken inside and someone mugs you for your wallet? You'd probably be too ashamed to go to the police. Even so, after I got to the end of the road it was as if my willpower had been mysteriously cancelled out. Something took control of my hands, I did a three-pointer at the end of the street, and came back down. I found myself stopping beside her, and winding down the window. It was all against my better judgement, and I could feel palpitations in my chest, and sweat forming on my temples. It occurred to me that I would probably be too anxious to manage anything anyhow.

I looked at her and she looked at me, and I tried to say something, but nothing came out. She said, 'Yes?'

I wasn't sure of the formula, so I said, 'Have you got

the time?' because that was suitably ambiguous. She looked at her watch, shook her wrist and put it to her ear. She said, 'Sorry, it stopped. I get bad luck with watches.'

She had a nice voice. It was soft and melodious, with quite a strong accent that I couldn't place.

I tried again, and said, 'Are you working?'

She looked at me with a puzzled expression, and then enlightenment dawned. A whole gallery of expressions crossed her face one after the other, from indignation to delight. Finally she laughed and put her hand to her mouth in a way that was really very sweet and charming. 'Oh,' she said. 'Oh, you think I'm bad girl.'

I was appalled, and started gabbling, 'Oh, I'm so sorry, really I'm very sorry, I didn't know, I thought, oh dear, I am so sorry, it's so embarrassing, forgive me, please forgive me, a horrible mistake, a horrible mistake.'

She continued laughing, and I just sat there in my car with my ears burning. At that point I should have driven away, but for some reason I didn't. She stopped giggling, and then to my surprise she opened the passenger door and got in, bringing with her a tidal wave of heavy perfume that I found very unpleasant and stifling. It reminded me of my grandmother in old age, attempting to disguise the odours of incontinence.

The woman sat next to me and looked at me with a pert expression. She had dark brown eyes and had her shiny black hair done in the kind of style that I believe is called a bob. It suited her very well. As I said, she was a well-built girl, with wide hips and large breasts. She wasn't the sort I would normally have taken a fancy to.

'I called cab,' she said, 'but it didn't come, and I waited

long, long time, so you can take me home, but I regret I don't sleep with you just now.'

'Oh,' I said.

'It's not far,' she said, 'just few streets, but I don't like to walk. This place is full of bad ones, bloody allsorts.'

I was shocked. I said, 'You shouldn't be getting into cars with strange men. Something might happen.'

She shot me a contemptuous look and said, 'You wanted me in your car just before, when you thought I was bad girl. Before you didn't tell me not to go getting in car.'

I said, 'Yes, but –'

And she interrupted me with a wave of her hand: 'But nothing. No bullshits now. I live down that way. You give me lift and that's how you say sorry. And you protect me from other strange men. OK, let's go.'

I delivered her to a place that doesn't exist any more. It wasn't far from that bridge at the top of the hill where alcoholics from the drying-out clinic used to commit suicide by throwing themselves down to the road below. It was a whole street of semi-derelict terraces that must have been grand once, but back then it was full of abandoned cars and litter. Not many houses had intact window frames, and nothing can have been painted for years. There were wide cracks in many of the walls, and you could see that there were tiles missing or broken on almost every roof. All the same, it seemed quite a friendly and unthreatening sort of place, and that was indeed what it turned out to be. It was a street full of poor people and transients who wanted to live in peace and for whom decorating would have been expensive and pointless. It all got demolished and redeveloped during the Thatcher era. I was sad about that, but it needed doing, I suppose. I passed by when they were wrecking it, and I asked the demolition men for the street sign. I've still got it somewhere in the garage.

When I stopped the car she held out her right hand very formally, and said, 'Roza. Nice to meet you. Thank you for the lift. I hope you find someone nice to sleep with.'

I took her hand and shook it. I thought I ought to give her a false name, but couldn't think of one. I was embarrassed by my name anyway. I'm not from a well-to-do family, and I always thought it sounded pretentious. 'I'm Christian,' I said, having been reduced by confusion into telling the truth.

'Christian?' she repeated. I suppose it must have been a name that she thought didn't suit me.

'My parents thought it sounded posh. Everyone calls me Chris.'

Just before she left she leaned down to the window and smiled at me seriously, 'So, Chris, how much were you going to give me?'

'Give you?'

'For the sex, you know?'

'Oh,' I said, 'I don't know. I don't know what . . . I have no idea . . .'

'So, Chris, you never been with bad girl before?'

'No, I haven't.' She looked at me with sceptical indulgence, and I felt my ears begin to burn again.

Roza said, 'They all say that. Every one. Not one man has ever been with bad girl before. Never never never.'

I was thinking over the startling implications of this

when she added, 'When I was bad girl I never took less than five hundred. I didn't do cheap.'

With that, she turned and climbed the tilting steps to her door. She waved at me gently, with a strangely old-fashioned circular movement of her hand, and before she went in she said, 'You come by sometime and I give you coffee maybe, I don't know.'

I just sat there for a while with the motor turning, and the Archway rain began to fall more heavily. I'd worked out by then that Roza must indeed have been a prostitute, but wasn't any more. I wondered if I had offended her at all, or if I had merely amused her. It felt as though she had been teasing me.

I don't know how to classify my falling in love with Roza. I've been in love often enough to be completely exhausted by it, and not to know what it means any more. When you look back afterwards, you can always find another way of putting it. You say, 'I was obsessed, it was really lust, I was fooling myself,' because after you've recovered from being in love, you always decide that that wasn't what it was.

Every time you fall in love it's a bit different, and in any case love is a word that gets used too lightly. It ought to be a sacred word that's hardly ever used. But it was then when I was sitting there in my car with the engine running and the wipers slapping that I began at the very least to fall into fascination. You can call it love, if that's what suits. I think that that's what I would call it.

2

The Man in the Shit-brown Allegro

When I went out it was just one of my strange urges.

I didn't need any money and I'd never tried getting it from streetwalking. Perhaps I was bored. I used to get bored with myself sometimes. I'd get this feeling that I ought to be running down mountains and singing, like in *The Sound of Music*, waving my arms about and being joyful, and instead I'd realise that I was sitting in front of a quiz show in a condemned building, smoking cigarettes and drinking black coffee that made me feel bitter in my mouth. It wasn't my ideal life. So I'd get an impulse to do something to put the flavours back on my tongue.

Pretending to be a streetwalker is something that maybe you'd do with a friend at university when you were a bit drunk and hysterical, and then when the first car drew up alongside, you'd run away laughing, and shouting, 'Oh my God, oh my God.'

I did it this time because I suppose I'm not exactly normal anyway, and besides, I don't even know if any of us understand our own reasons. The important thing wasn't what was happening in my head, but what I went out and did. I put on tarty clothes – a short skirt with glittery gold threads, and some high-heeled white boots, and a little blouse. I had some disgusting perfume that some hopeful cheapskate had given me once. I'd had it for years, and every time I sniffed it, I thought, 'This must be eau de streetwalker.' I splashed it on and practically made myself dizzy. I thought, 'Why not?' and made my face up like I was some vamp from a French novel. I even had some weird lipstick.

When I went out it occurred to me that my neighbours would notice what I was up to, but the fact is that it wasn't a neighbourhood in any proper sense. All the houses were condemned, and we were all tramps. The place was full of do-it-yourself revolutionaries, hippies, guys who played bass with imaginary bands, scarecrows, girls in ethnic skirts, amateur dope dealers, actors adrift, 1970s orphans with troubled minds and vague big ideas, all looking for the authentic life and wishing they were really in New York, hobnobbing with Andy Warhol and Lou Reed, or in Paris throwing cobblestones at the CRS. In my house there was a Jewish actor, there was a boy pretending to be someone else, but who really wanted to be Bob Dylan, and there was a sculptress who made little ceramic things. There wasn't anyone on the top floor because there wasn't a roof to speak of. The Bob Dylan used to build car engines up there.

I dare say there were some real ordinary citizens in the neighbourhood, but I didn't know any. There wasn't anyone there who I'd feel reluctant to startle, but even so, I went a couple of streets away, because in London every street is a village, and you only know the people in your own street.

I think that while I stood there play-acting the street-walker, leaning against a corner and smoking, and showing off my legs, I wasn't really expecting anyone to stop. It wasn't a red-light district, so why would anyone kerb-crawl by? I felt quite safe, just enjoying the fantasy, and doing a role-play, like in a drama class. It started to drizzle a bit, and I was thinking of packing it in, but I couldn't stand the thought of going back in and watching more quiz shows while I waited for my life to amount to something, so I stood there imagining what it was like to have to stand out in the rain, really doing this job to keep body and soul together. I was watching the litter blowing about, and thinking that it might have been pretty if only it wasn't rubbish. I noticed two rats, and I watched them for a while. Back then, it was a happy time for rats, because no one was collecting the rubbish.

When a shabby brown car went past me and did a U-turn, I was completely unprepared. The poor man was very embarrassed, and for a few moments I didn't even realise that he was trying to pick me up. As soon as he spoke to me I forgot what I'd been pretending to be, and told him my watch didn't work very well. When I started to realise what he was thinking, I was half-way between embarrassed and entertained. I was pleased that my ruse was successful, but then I was horrified by what I could have got myself into.

Fortunately he was a very nice man, the kind you like immediately, someone a bit like me, who would have been better suited to more exciting times, and was whiling away an ordinary life in resignation. He said his name was Christian, which struck me as funny for a man trying to pick up a streetwalker, but then I never did notice religion having any good effect on anyone. Look what it did to my country. Everyone called him Chris, he said, which seemed reasonable to me. I called him Chris until I came up with a pet name.

Chris was in his forties, quite slim and not very tall. He had a broad forehead and some wispy hair on top, and nice big teeth which gave him a wide and friendly smile. He was humorous and serious all at once. He wore a business suit that was rumpled from so much driving about for his job, and he had the air of someone who didn't really belong in a suit anyway. I thought he would have liked to have been twenty years younger, dressed up in jeans and headbanging next to the speakers at Who concerts. I'd say he was forlornly forty. That's young and sad enough to be attractive to a younger woman.

I invited him to drop me home, and he was horrified at the thought of my being willing to get in a car with a strange man. He was an innocent, really. When I said goodbye to him, I asked him to come and visit me sometime. I could tell he was harmless, and there's nothing like living in London to make you lonely and turn you into a ghost. The only person I used to talk to was the guy upstairs who played and sang Dylan songs all the time. I told him my stories so many times and from so many angles that I lost track of everything I'd said.

Anyway, the truth is that I felt sympathy between us.

I didn't like the thought of never seeing him again, and I regretted telling him that I was really worth five hundred pounds. I didn't know it at the time, but it was the most destructive thing I could have told him.

3
The Princess on the Dungheap

When I went back I had the vague idea that Roza might sleep with me one day.

Well, that's the truth of the matter, but I didn't really believe that there was any prospect of it. I was a reluctant travelling salesman with a daughter at university and a mortgage on a medium-sized house in Sutton. I was driving all over the place in a shit-brown Austin Allegro, carrying a freight of pharmaceuticals and medical hardware that I had to sell to doctors. You didn't get enough of a turnover to earn the kinds of commission that made 'bad girls' a feasible proposition. Even so, I started to put money away, five pounds at a time, sometimes ten.

Nowadays I look back and think how sordid that was, and I still wince at the memory. I have three excuses, however. One is that I was married to the Great White Loaf, and the second is that I don't think I ever seriously intended to offer Roza five hundred pounds for sex. It was a sort of backup for the eventuality of life getting so lonely that there was no other prospect of consolation. It was like a ninety-year-old buying a pair of weighted boots just in case he has the chance one day of going to the moon. My third excuse is that after so many years of being undesired, it didn't seem possible that anyone could possibly want me unless there was an extra incentive. I didn't have any confidence any more.

I never lost the sexual attraction I felt for Roza, even long after we became friends. If anything, it increased because she began to touch my heart. It was like the yeast in the bread or the pepper sauce on the steak. There's been a little nip of sexual attraction with any woman I've ever been friends with. I used to dream about having sex with Roza, and sometimes I still do. Old men don't become virtuous just because age pins them up against a wall and snarls contempt into their ears. Time screws death into you through every orifice, but it never stops you yearning.

I don't know what I was expecting when I knocked on her door after seeing Dr Patel in Davenant Road. I'd tried the bell, but it was obviously disconnected, and I was thinking about how stupid I was being, at the same time as I was rapping on the door with my knuckles. I remember that the Vietnamese had just invaded Cambodia, because I'd heard about it on the car radio when I was turning the corner of the street.

I was surprised when the door was opened by a young man in jeans and bare feet. He had tousled curly hair and the air of someone who normally concentrated upon higher things. He didn't seem at all surprised to see me. I said, 'Is Roza in?'

'No idea,' he said. He was quite well spoken. 'I'll go and look.'

He went a little way up the corridor and knocked

on a door. 'Hey, Roza, there's someone here to see you.'

'She's in,' he said, giving me a businesslike smile, and then he disappeared into another room. I distinctly heard him locking his door, and there came the sound of that kind of music that I believe they used to call 'psychedelic'. I was about forty years old back then and I had no idea at all what the youngsters were listening to, or even talking about. It used to make me feel I was being left out and that I was already past it. Now that I'm truly old, I don't even care. All the stuff they take so seriously is just ephemera. I look at youngsters nowadays and mostly feel sorry for them, and the ones I don't pity can go and jump in the lake. Still, at the age of forty I was young enough to feel young, but old enough to feel left out. There'd been a revolution and I'd missed it, and I didn't even know precisely what the revolution was about. I just knew that my daughter wasn't remotely like my sisters when they were her age, and fortunately she wasn't like the Great White Loaf either.

Roza came out of her room and didn't recognise me for a moment. I said, 'It's Chris, remember? You offered me coffee.'

'Oh yes. Chris. Well, OK, why not? You come downstairs.'

I followed her, and was amazed by that extraordinary house. Great slabs of plaster had fallen off the walls, exposing the grey laths underneath. There weren't any lampshades, and the wiring was that maroon-coloured plaited stuff that must have pre-dated the war. It was just hanging off the walls in festoons. The floorboards were partly missing, so you had to be careful where you put your feet, and one whole step was missing from the staircase that went down into the basement. There weren't any carpets to speak of, except for a grey one in the basement that was stiff with grease because that's where the cooker was. The cooker was streaked all over with dark yellow and brown solidified sploshes of antediluvian fat. There was a gas fire down there too, and some unstuffed armchairs, and it was in those armchairs, face to face across the gas fire, that Roza seduced my spirit and unleashed on me the stories of her life.

She was like the Ancient Mariner in that poem, who used to buttonhole people and not let them go until the tale was over, except that in this case I never wanted to get away. As I said, I had fallen into fascination. I liked to watch her talking, even when I wasn't listening, because she'd told me all the same things many times before. When I wasn't concentrating on what she was saying, I was looking at her body and her mouth and her face, imagining that we were in bed, imagining what they could do to me.

She didn't disclose very much on that first visit. We drank coffee in our armchairs and she questioned me a little, and then she offered to show me round the house, as a respectable woman does who has guests who have come for the first time.

The rest of the house was just as ramshackle as the bit I had already seen. The top floor was uninhabited because the roof leaked, and in one of the rooms an engine was being rebuilt on a Workmate. Roza said that it was the project of the young man who lived on the first floor and had a job in a garage. I encountered him lots of times, and I would say that he was one of those misguided middle-class boys who thought that slumming it was the authentic way of life. He used to sing Bob Dylan songs in his room, and his not unpleasant caterwauling and strumming would drift through the house like the soundtrack to the story that I was in with Roza. My daughter used to play Bob Dylan records on her gramophone, and I got to like it even though I complained, and that was how I recognised the songs that the youngster was bashing out. I expect he was lonely and was hoping to be a star one day. The Bob Dylan upstairs was supposed to be somebody called John Horrocks, but the real John Horrocks had gone to Katmandu to be a hippy, and the Bob Dylan had taken over his name to save the bother of registering the new details with the landlord. The only things about the real John Horrocks that I ever found out were that he usually had several lovers and that he had enormous feet, because he'd left a pair of moccasins in the middle of the kitchen floor, and that was where they stayed for as long as I was a visitor, unless the Bob Dylan was wearing them. As for the Bob Dylan Upstairs, I never did discover his real name. I started to refer to him as the BDU, and very soon Roza did too.

There was another fellow there who was apparently an actor, and Roza used to laugh about him because she said he was the one Jew she'd ever met who was really as mean as Jews were supposed to be. He was the only one in the house with a telephone, and he would put one of those locks through the hole in the dial, so that no one else could use it. He had a pretty blonde actress girlfriend who used to arrive in a small red

Renault, and the sound of them repeatedly making love would resonate through the house, mixing up with the sound of Bob Dylan songs and Roza's musical voice. I liked the honesty of noisy lovemaking. I didn't grow up amid that kind of honesty. I am embarrassed by it, though. The Great White Loaf would never have made a squeak even if there were no one else within a hundred miles.

The last resident was a young woman that I hardly ever saw. She was a pretty sculptress who dressed in dungarees, and she used to make clay slabs in the shape of sails, and put them in the Thames at low tide in order to take photographs of them. She wore one of those badges that said 'A woman needs a man like a fish needs a bicycle', but the reason I hardly ever saw her was that she spent almost all the time at her boyfriend's house. That was the seventies and early eighties for you.

To this forty-year-old it all felt as if I had been secretly flung into the centre of the Alternative Society, as we used to call it, except that the revolution fizzled out and never went anywhere in the end. It was quite nice at the time, though. I didn't feel so left out, although I was frightened of the disorder. When punk appeared and all the hippies vanished, that was when I finally realised there was no point trying to join in. Middle age makes you dignified, and if it doesn't, then you're a sad case. Sometimes you'd see a middle-aged punk, and you'd just think, 'How pitiful.' The only thing more pitiful than a middle-aged punk is a white Rastafarian. I did meet one of those once, and he was lonelier than I was.

It's funny how in those days all the marginal people

managed to make it seem as if it was the rest of us who'd really been marginalised. It was a neat trick. I didn't like knowing that all the youngsters thought I was boring, mostly because I suspected that it was true. What's sad about being boring, about being nobody in particular, is that it means you're the same as everyone else. You're just taking up space on this earth. Theoretically you could make up a certain poundage of sausages, and that's all you amount to. You're just flesh that exists for a while and then stops existing. I wonder now if it was those youngsters who were really the boring ones. At that time it did feel as if it were me, though.

Roza didn't find me boring. I was just what she needed. I was someone who drank her coffee and looked at her affectionately and listened to her stories, and then pecked her on the cheek when I left. She was very self-obsessed, which is usually a fault, but at least it prevented her from getting fed up with me, as I didn't really have to say very much.

On that day, after she'd shown me round the house, she made coffee on the sordid cooker, using one of those double-decker Italian contraptions, and we sat opposite each other in the armchairs. She lit the gas fire with a match which she then used to light a Black Russian. They were her favourite cigarettes, though she sometimes smoked Abdullahs. She sipped on her coffee, and blew smoke up to the yellow ceiling.

I didn't really know what to say, and she didn't seem to expect me to say anything. I was perplexed by her. She dressed in expensive clothes and smoked aristocratic cigarettes, and everything about her was immaculate, but she lived in that dirty hovel. She was like a princess perched on a dungheap.

'Where are you from?' I asked eventually.

'Yugoslavia,' she said. 'Actually, I'm a Serb.'

'I don't know much about Yugoslavia,' I said. 'Is it nice?'

She shrugged, 'It depends. Is England nice?'

We smiled at each other, and I said, 'Not at the moment.'

'What you want to know,' she said, 'is why I am living here, like this, in this dirty place.'

'I am curious,' I admitted.

'I pay five pounds a week for it.'

'Good God, that's cheap!'

'Not when the roof leaks. Anyway, it belongs to the Co-operative Housing, and one day they want to knock it down, so until then they rent it out at five pounds a week, and they call it "Hard to Let" housing, and the waiting list is years long.' She laughed at the irony of it.

'But that doesn't entirely explain why you're living here.'

She looked at me as if I was stupid and said, 'I am saving all my money. I want to do big things with it.'

'You have lots of money?'

'Like I told you, I was bad girl. Now I have enough, and anyway I got fed up, and I stopped. Now I am good girl again. I am resting.' She looked genuinely pleased with herself. 'Also,' she added, 'I don't really exist, so I have to hide, and this is good place. You know the boy upstairs? He pretend to be someone called John Horrocks, and I pretend to be Sharon Didsbury. The real ones were here before, and we take the rooms and the names to save doing it official. Too much trouble, too much paper.'

'You don't exist?' I asked. I thought she was making a metaphysical point about the state of her soul.

'No visa, no work permit,' she said. 'I am tiny little parasite.' She showed me how tiny she was by pinching a centimetre of air between thumb and forefinger.

'Haven't you got any qualifications?' I asked.

She looked offended. 'I got degree at Zagreb. Anyway, I started one.'

All I could think of to say was 'Oh.'

Then she said, 'I'm here because I made fuck-ups. Everything turns to shit. You know, I pick up potato and by the time it gets to my mouth, it's turned to shit, with horsehair in it. I got used to shit and horsehair in my teeth, no bullshits.'

Roza blew more smoke at the ceiling, and said philosophically, 'It's OK now. No more shit for Roza. Do you want to know?'

'Know?'

'About Roza who ate too much shit, and made fuck-ups? It's good for laughing.'

I shrugged. At that time I only wanted to sleep with her, really, but when you're fascinated by a woman you'll settle for her stories, because that's how you stay en route.

'My whole life, one shit thing after another,' she said, blowing out smoke and laughing. 'Still, you know, I like it when I think about it. It was my life, and I like it. I had adventures.'

4
This Father of Mine

My father was a partisan with Tito.

That's what I told him. I liked to talk about this father of mine. I never spoke harshly about him, and Chris found that surprising, in view of what I said about him. The thing is, if you want to seem to be interesting, you shouldn't be predictable.

I said my father had an eyepatch that made him resemble a pirate, and he had five bullets left in him from the war. Every year he went to the hospital for an X-ray, and he'd come back and pin it up against the kitchen window. He'd check up on the meandering of the bullets from one part of his body to another. What he was hoping was that one day they would start poking through his skin so that he could pull them out and keep them, all in a line on the mantelpiece. That was his ambition. He liked to say, 'One day one of these bullets might stray into my lungs, and I'd be dead, just like that,' and he'd raise an eyebrow and snap his thumb and forefinger.

He taught me a little routine about how he might die. I acted it out for Chris once when we'd had some wine and got a bit merry, and I was going on about my father again.

'OK,' I said, mimicking this father of mine, 'the bullet goes into my lungs, and I get a pain. It's a big pain. I put my hand to my chest, and I go, "Aahhhhh," and then I wave my hands, like this, and then I cough, Uh! Uh! Uh!, and suddenly I get blood out of my mouth, OK? It goes down my chin, and my mouth fills up, and I am coughing and coughing, and Mama comes out, OK? And she says, "Husband, you're spoiling that clean shirt that I just washed," and I am lying on the floor dying and Mama is sprinkling salt on the bloody shirt to try and soak it out.'

By then I was on that greasy floor pretending to die, with a cigarette in one hand and a glass of wine in the other. I said, 'And then my father he always said the same thing, he said, "They'll take me away wrapped up in the national flag, and I'll go and be made into meat pies at the factory, and Marshall Tito, he'll serve me up to the President of the United States who's come on a visit, and my bones they'll grind up and spread on the fields, and some bones will be made into glue for sticking books together, and that's how I'm going to be useful when I'm dead."'

Chris looked down at me, and there was real affection and enjoyment in his eyes, and he said, 'You did this every year when he came home with an X-ray?' and so I said, 'Also at parties for his friends.'

'You must have been a sweet little girl,' Chris said, and I replied, 'Even inside every damn fucked-up woman there's some sweet little girl.'

Chris said I should have been an actress, and it was a miracle that I'd managed to put on that dying act without spilling any wine.

I said that my father liked to frighten me by raising his eyepatch so that I could see the eyelid sunken into the socket, and then he'd chase me about the house pretending that his hands were claws, and making animal noises. After he'd done it enough times, it stopped frightening me, and it was just another game that ended in tickling. My friends and my brother's friends never stopped being impressed by the eye socket, however.

Chris liked me telling these tales about my father. He was a patient person and he thought that I really needed to talk about this other man who was such a big thing in my life. I kept telling him these stories as if they were the most important in the world, and he sat in the filthy armchair and sipped my coffee and just looked at me with his eyes full of pleasure. I probably could have been saying anything at all. I'd hooked him almost straight away, and I was giving myself a problem, wondering what to do with him now that I had him dangling on the line. I had to think about what it was that I wanted from Chris.

'My father was like a mountain,' I said. 'He was a monolith. He was somewhat awe-inspiring . . . He could eat enormous piles of food and never get fat, and he sat at mealtimes with his fork and knife in his fists, and just talked about the war. He was like a lot of people of his generation. The war came, and then afterwards the survivors could never stop talking about it because they were so amazed to be still alive. He was fond of saying, "My life is a damn epilogue, and the epilogue's a whole lot longer than the damn story." He'd raise his glass and say, "Here's to a long and happy epilogue, and here's to all the poor bastards who didn't make it . . ."'

I told Chris I was brought up to be a communist. If you were Yugoslavian you had to be, back then, in the same way that some people have to be Muslim or Catholic, just because of the accidents of birth. I didn't have to know much about it. In London in those days lots of people were going around saying they were communists. A certain kind of person thought it made them seem heroic. Archway was full of communist factions that truly despised each other. In Yugoslavia we used to have a saying that when communists had to make up a firing squad, they formed a circle. Anyway, nobody believes any of it any more, but back then in Archway we had the Revolutionary Communist Party, the Communist Party of Great Britain, the International Marxist Group, the Socialist Workers Party, every possible kind of revolutionary and socialist this and that, and then there were various kinds of anarchists. Everyone knew that half the people at the meetings were from the British secret services, and they were just spying on each other. Nobody with any sense believes any of it any more. I wouldn't bother now, but I did defend Tito. It was a matter of being loyal. Chris never argued with me about it very much, and I bet he was really a Conservative. He once told me he was a Liberal, and even put up the posters in his window and went canvassing. When he was faced with that box in the polling station, though, I bet his little cross went beside the name of the Conservative. He moaned like everyone else when the Conservatives got in, but you couldn't help noticing that even though Mrs Thatcher won three elections you hardly ever met anyone who admitted having voted for her.

My father was a proper communist though, an out-and-out Stalinist, and it didn't do him too much good after the war, when it turned out that Tito wanted to do things his own way. My dad was like a sailing ship that gets a great start in a race because there's a brisk wind, and then the wind drops and all the rowing boats overtake.

My father was fifteen when the war started, and at first he joined the Cetniks on the Ravna Gora plateau. I don't know how much of this meant anything to Chris. He just wanted to be with me, and I could see he was happy admiring my body and listening to my voice. I liked it because it made me feel like a hot girl.

Anyway, the Cetniks were royalists and the royal family was in London at that time, I believe. My father had fun with the Cetniks to begin with. It was a big adventure, wading through mud, swinging on ropes, crawling through pipes, sticking bayonets in sandbags.

The trouble was that he didn't give a damn about the King, so it was difficult being a royalist. The Cetnik officers were all Hapsburgish aristocratic types, and they liked their drills and their polishing. Meanwhile, the men were getting into feuds with each other, like proper Balkan bandits, and the officers didn't know how to keep discipline, and so one day he defected to the communist partisans because he was fed up with skulking in the forest with a bunch of disputatious royalists.

There were plenty of people to fight. The place was crawling with Romanians, Bulgarians, Italians, Germans and Hungarians, and there were some Croatians who became Nazis too. If you want to speak insultingly about

Croatians you just refer to them as Ustase. When they want to insult Serbs, they call them Cetniks.

There was a lot of talk and rumour. People were saying that the Cetniks were colluding with the Nazis to wipe out the communists, and even collaborating with the Ustase. The Ustase liked to get rid of Serbs, Jews and Gypsies by drowning them. They had an extermination camp at Jazenovac that was even condemned by the Gestapo for its cruelty. I heard that 1.7 million Yugoslavs died in the war, and one million of the deaths were fratricide. We didn't need Germans and Italians to come and kill us, because we could manage it on our own, thank you. Chris said, 'Hey, Roza, I'm going to have to stay on your sweet side,' and I said, 'Balkan girls have a big sweet side.'

My father defected to the communists when he was supposed to be taking part in an attack on them. He made sure he was out on the edge of the flank, and when the column approached he slipped away and joined them, and told them about the impending attack. So they ambushed the ambushers, and my father helped to wipe out his former comrades. During the battle he got the tip of a bayonet in the eye, and so he had to learn to shoot left-handed. It was quite a romance.

The communists were pretty successful as resistance fighters. They even set up schools, and rifle and cigarette factories. They were fighting not only the Italians and the Germans, but the other resistance groups as well, except that towards the end of the war enough Italians changed sides to form a whole battalion that fought for us.

I knew a great deal about the Second World War in

Yugoslavia. It was an area of expertise that I had, because of university, and I was quite clear about who was who and what was what, and when everything happened, but I've no doubt that Chris was having trouble following it. He said it was very interesting, and he said his wife had got puzzled by the reading matter at his bedside. Before he mostly used to read Louis L'Amour novels and DIY magazines, but now he had started reading the books about Tito and Fitzroy Maclean that I was lending him.

It was fun telling Chris gory details, such as that my father once had to eat his own horse, and Tito's life was once saved because his dog took all the force of a bomb that fell beside him, and that collaborators used to get thrown out of trucks with their first finger cut off at first joint, the second finger at the second joint, and the third and fourth fingers cut off altogether. They'd sever the tendons of the thumb and staple their lips together, plus the other lips if they were women.

He used to shudder and say how awful this was, but I didn't see it. I thought they deserved it, and I said, 'I hate people like that.' I have the attitudes of an amazon, and maybe that made me even more wonderful for Chris.

Chris said, 'I don't hate anyone. I couldn't be bothered. I think my wife hates me, though.'

I said, 'I hate lots of people,' and when he raised his eyebrows in enquiry, I numbered them off on my fingers. 'I hate Croatians, Albanians, Muslims, Russians, and Bosnians, if they're not Serbs. And there's an Englishman I hated, but he died, so that's OK. I'll tell you sometime.'

He looked puzzled and said something like, 'You don't strike me as a wholesale hater. You can't hate such an awful lot of people. It's unmanageable. It takes up too much emotion. It's bad enough being hated. Nothing makes you feel so weary as living with someone who hates you.'

And I replied, 'Oh, it's OK, I like Slovenians and Montenegrins. And maybe Greeks. At least Greeks are Orthodox.'

'Who was the Englishman?' Chris asked.

'I'll tell you sometime, but maybe not yet. You know, I like it, being the daughter of a partisan. I say to myself, "Hey, Roza, you're a partisan's daughter." That's how I explain myself when I think about me and I wonder why I'm doing things. I'm not the same as everyone else, because I'm a partisan's daughter.'

'Your father seems very important to you,' Chris said to me, in his bland fashion, and I shrugged and replied, 'Sure. For every little girl, her father is the first one she falls in love with.'

'I don't think my daughter was ever in love with me,' Chris said. 'I wonder what was wrong with me.'

I said, 'You never got a chance to be a partisan.'

I felt sorry for Chris. Actually he was very vulnerable, and here I was playing games with him, even tormenting him a bit, and it was amusing, and I laughed at him, but not with any cruelty. I leaned forward in my armchair and blew out a cloud of smoke. 'I tell you something else,' I said. 'My papa was the first one I slept with.'

Chris didn't know how to react to that. He was shocked. His eyes went wide. But I was smiling, and it confused him. In the end he said, 'I'm so sorry. I'm so sorry.'

'Why sorry?'

'Well, it must have been terrible. To have your father do that to you. I can't imagine how bad it must be.'

'You're funny,' I said, enjoying myself. 'It was like I said. Papa is the first man you fall in love with.'

'Even so . . . to do that to your daughter?'

It was fun. I breathed out more smoke, and stubbed out my cigarette. I went over and knelt before him where he was sitting. He practically jumped, looking scared and delighted at the same time, and it occurred to me that he might be thinking that I was about to do something.

But I beckoned for him to lean down, and I put my lips next to his ear. I could smell his aftershave. It was that Old Spice stuff. I wanted to charm and shock him. I giggled, and then whispered 'He didn't do it to me. It wasn't poor Roza. It was poor Papa. It was me. I took my daddy into bed and I got him to do it.'

I leaned back and watched the reaction on his face.

5
The Girl from Belgrade

Roza told me that she was born in a little village near Belgrade, not far from the Danube, and quite close to Avala. There's a huge monument there, to the Unknown Soldier. The climate is extreme and often hostile, and people dream about the Dalmatian coast in the same way that cold Americans are supposed to dream about California. Just across the Dinaric mountains it's more like Italy; a land of wine, olives, figs, aromatic shrubs and Aleppo pines. I went there several times later on, but before Yugoslavia fell apart. It was a kind of pilgrimage.

Around Belgrade, people suffocate in the heat of the summer. The road tar gets sticky and glutinous, the leaves wither on the trees, fires light themselves in the fields, and mirages shimmer above any patch of flat ground. There's an old fortress called Kalemegdan, and it's a relief to go in there and cool down in the great stone rooms. There are thunderstorms so immense that water runs off the ground in sudden floods because it can't soak into the baked earth, and you get floods caused by the melting of the Alpine ice. It wells up from under the ground and fills lakes even in places where there's been no rain. People have to work continually on the irrigation canals, not just to keep the land watered, but to prevent the settlements from submerging.

Roza said that her father hated the thunder because to him it sounded like an artillery attack. He would go into a kind of rage, and she and her mother would lie sweating upstairs with the electricity prickling on their skin. He would go out into the torrential downpours and stagger about, shaking his fist, shouting, and firing both barrels of his shotgun into the sky. I said, 'That must have been worrying,' and Roza said, 'No, it was just my papa.' Once her mother went out to try to bring him in, and he accidentally struck her on the cheek with the butt of the gun, so that it came up in a terrible livid bruise, and after that she left him alone to rage in the thunder showers. The day after the accident he came home with a ring for his wife and a doll for Roza, and he said, 'I try to control it, but it's difficult sometimes.' Roza said that she thought he was going to cry, because his lower lip was trembling and his eyes were moist. I can't imagine my own father crying. British fathers don't weep in front of their children. Her mother said to her, 'Printzeza, whatever your father does, remember that he is a brave man who has been to hell and stayed there for a while, and then come back again.'

In the summer they would yearn for the icy winds that come in from Hungary, but in winter when the Hungarian wind was sawing everything in half, and they were floundering about in the snow, they would long for the roasting of summer. Only in the spring and autumn was it possible to live a life that wasn't a hostage to the climate.

More importantly, in that region it isn't ever possible not to live a hostage to history. They're all possessed and tormented by it. It takes the logic and humanity out of their souls and gives them heroic stupidity.

6
The Secret Policeman

After he was a partisan, my father was a secret policeman.

That's what I told Chris. I liked to tease him with more and more stories about my father, because he was fascinated by the idea that I slept with him and wasn't bothered about it. I kept him in suspense by telling him a lot of other things about my father first.

The truth is that I was getting very fond of Chris, he was becoming a dependable and happy part of my life, I looked forward to his visits, and every day I made myself look nice and thought about what I'd say, just in case he turned up after seeing Dr Patel or one of the other doctors. I thought that if I kept from telling him about all the details of the incest for a while, he'd keep coming back. Once I'd divulged them, I'd be forced to tell him the other stories.

So I told him that after he was a partisan, my father was a secret policeman. In those days the secret police was called UDBA. In 1966 it turned out that they'd had listening devices even in Tito's own office, and he realised why it was that his plans were always getting blocked. He subjected it to a reform from which it never recovered, but just after the war it did help to keep Tito in power, making sure that Yugoslavia didn't fall apart again.

My father had a busy time, because there were hundreds of war criminals on the loose, plus a great many people who were conveniently considered to be so; fascist Ustase from Croatia, royalist Cetniks from Serbia, Albanians from Kosovo who were just a general nuisance and wouldn't cooperate with anyone. I said that one of my father's first jobs was to help gather evidence against the Cetnik commander, Mijailovic, and he was also involved in the prosecution of Archbishop Stepinac, a Croatian who had busied himself with suppressing Serbian orthodoxy. Everyone said he was a Vatican stooge.

In the ten years after the war Tito was imposing strong party discipline, and wasn't allowing any latitude. That was when the ideological enemies were being pursued. Now that communism's all washed up, it seems odd to remember all those class enemies; revanchists, recidivists, liberals, reactionaries, a big list of traitors. My father particularly disdained the bourgeoisie, and anything that irritated him, such as a wheelbarrow whose wheel had fallen off, or his beloved car when it broke down, would be denounced as a petit bourgeois reactionary. It was just snobbery really.

I said to Chris, 'My father was always certain about everything,' and I was laughing about it.

Chris said, 'That's probably where you get it from.'

It's true that I'm opinionated. I believe in good and evil, and I know which is which, and I know that sometimes you do evil to do good. Chris was more subtle than me. You could just see him longing to tell me that life was more complicated than that, and restraining himself because it's bad English manners to patronise, and back then it was getting extra dangerous to patronise women. Men got their balls bitten off.

I'd already realised that Chris wanted to sleep with me, but I wasn't sure what to do. He'd got off on the wrong foot by trying to pick me up when he thought I was a streetwalker, and I'd got off on the wrong foot by telling him I was worth five hundred pounds. He was married with a daughter, too. Not that I was particularly worried. He said that a wife eventually becomes a sister or an enemy, and I knew for sure he was right about that. It was what every married man used to tell me. It's one of nature's jokes, making most men out of fire and most women out of earth. Chris said that his wife had skimmed milk in her veins instead of blood.

I was trying to work out whether Chris was falling in love with me, and what it would be like if I were his wife or his mistress. I was frightened that if I slept with him he might not come back. It was a big risk.

7
Bivouac on a Bombsite

I suppose that if you have clear beliefs it helps you to fight and survive a war, and then endure the memories afterwards. That's probably what got Roza's father through it. My father got through it by being an old-fashioned patriot. When I think about Roza being a communist, I remind myself that for a long time it was very easy to be one, because for such a long time the communists managed to conceal the fact that their system was an economic and humanitarian catastrophe. It was one of the greatest and longest self-deceptions in history, and you can't blame people for falling for it when none of us is any good at perceiving the present, let alone the future. It might even be wrong to suppose that Yugoslav communism actually failed. It more or less worked for a long time, by sitting on everyone equally heavily, and then it just stopped. I thought that Roza's communism was very like the Catholicism of someone who crosses themselves when they pass a church, but never goes into one, and who doesn't know anything about theology. When I suggested this idea to her, she admitted that I was probably right.

The problem for Roza's father was that Tito really did believe in the eventual withering away of the state.

He gave workers control of factories and permitted the republics greater autonomy, and Roza's father thought it was a terrible mistake. He found himself more and more sidelined, and he had fewer and fewer important things to do. Apparently he fell into melancholy, and was sometimes very angry. Roza thought that in addition, he eventually started to feel remorse for things he had done in the war.

I don't know if he felt remorse about anything else. Roza said that as a father he'd behaved in a way that seemed pretty outrageous to me, but she herself wasn't at all bothered. In fact she even seemed pleased about it. Now that so many years have passed, I can still hear her voice going through my mind like a record that repeats itself over and over, romanticising about her father. I always loved the sound of her accent.

'My father was very tall and thin, and he had dark skin and he looked like a proper Slav. He had one eye left, that's all, but it used to burn all on its own, and with that eye he saw the future of the world that was going to be beautiful, and with it he looked with anger on anyone who was going to stand in the way. Someone knocked out two teeth with a steel helmet during the war, and he had gold ones that sparkled and made him look sinister and romantic. When I was little we had a game which was like a pirate taking over a ship, and I would make him stand in the garden, and I would climb up him, and when I was at the top I peeled up his top lip and made him face the sun, and I was delighted by the way his teeth flashed, and he said, "What'll we do when I die?" and I said, "We'll take out your teeth and sell them and we'll be rich forever," and he'd say, "What a

horrid Printzeza you are," and he'd swing me round and round and round till I thought I was going to be sick, and then he'd be dizzy and fall down, and I would jump on him and kiss his face.

'He met my mother at the great victory parade on 27 May 1945, which was when the partisans marched into Belgrade with the Red Army.'

She laid a circlet of flowers about his neck, and he took her hand and kissed her on the lips. It was all very romantic, and fully consonant with the general euphoria of the times. She spent the night with him in a bivouac on a bombsite, and Roza said it might have been because in those days only the partisans had a reliable source of food, and other people were even eating grass. That one night stretched into decades, not least because Roza's brother soon made his presence evident. He was called Friedrich, but Roza hardly ever mentioned him.

She said she wished that her parents had never been married. They weren't compatible. She was an old-fashioned orthodox Christian and that didn't go down very well with the atheist ex-partisan. Roza thought that he married her perhaps because of honour, or because he wanted a housewife for the dilapidated farmhouse that the party gave him. Perhaps she in her turn thought that life would be easier as the wife of a rising star in the party. In any case, everyone rushes into fecundity after a war.

She had apparently been a striking young woman with black eyes, dark hair and sensual lips, which is not how Roza remembered her, because it wasn't long before she was grey and worn out. She had a problem with chewing and sucking on her own lips, so that they would bleed, and she had a preoccupation with trying to get around the house as quietly as possible. It occurred to me that she must have been mentally ill, but Roza's opinion was that you had to be a lot madder than that.

They had been happy to begin with. He was delighted with his son, and she had enjoyed being a housewife, up until the time that the boy was old enough to go to school. Then she decided that she wanted to get work and become a teacher, but he couldn't agree. He thought it reflected badly on him if his wife went out to work, and he thought there was enough to do at home anyway. The fact was that she did not want any more children, and she wanted money of her own. He, on the other hand, had grown up in a huge family that was a positive deluge of brothers, sisters, cousins, uncles, aunts and relations so distant that no one could work out the details of consanguinity any more. Of this happy clan he was the sole survivor, as they had all perished at the hands of the Bulgarian Army, and no doubt he wished to recreate the conditions of his early life. He did not want her to use contraception, and Roza said she thought that her parents' sexual relations degenerated into something like rape. She'd lie awake at night listening to the thuds and raised voices from their room, without understanding what it was all about. Roza thought that her mother probably had several abortions, because sometimes she was in bed for days at a time, and a grandmother would come to look after the children. Perhaps Roza's father knew what his wife had done, but hadn't been able to prove it.

There was one night when it all boiled over, and her father lashed out. Roza was standing in the doorway of the bedroom, and she saw her father strike her mother across the mouth, so that she spun backwards into the corridor and fell heavily to the floor of the landing at the top of the stairs. She hit her head on the banister.

Roza was very small at the time, but she said that she always remembered vividly the horror of thinking that her mother was dead. She soon got up, however, but her two front teeth were broken and had gashed the insides of her lip, so that blood was running out of the corners of her mouth. She put her hands to her face and ran downstairs and into the garden.

At that point Roza attacked her father. He was standing absolutely still, appalled by what he had just done, and Roza flew at him, and flailed at him with her fists. She was trying to scream, but she couldn't make a sound. She was hammering at his thighs with all her strength, and when he put a hand down to stop her, she bit it. When she left Yugoslavia, he still had the scars of her teethmarks on his hands. He'd show her the marks and say, 'Look how you punished your daddy, little Printzeza.'

Roza said that the incident was the end of all the love in the marriage. He was contrite, but the mother was embittered and hardened, and consequently he found reasons to stay away from home. He'd be back for weekends and holidays, and slept in the spare room, exhausted by unhappiness, anger and guilt.

To begin with Roza thought it was her fault that her father had gone away, and she'd bitten her own hand to punish herself. She tried to show me the scar once, but I couldn't see anything. However, her father was soon giving all his affection to her and there was something about his resigned sadness that made her pity him, and made him approachable. She said that she and her father began falling in love very early in her life, and it was just something that happened, like an earthquake, or a tree falling down.

As for me, I sat listening to all this, to the rhythm of her voice with its strange accent, husky with smoke, and I felt a charge passing through me almost all the time. I couldn't help imagining what had happened with her father, and the mental images agitated me. They played themselves on a loop at night when I was trying to go to sleep. I also thought that it might have made her attracted to older men, and that might be to my advantage. It occurred to me in a moment of hopeful stupidity that I could sell my car and get a cheaper second-hand one, and put the money towards the five hundred pounds that by now I realised I wasn't ever going to offer her. I didn't do it, of course. I wasn't quite stupid enough. I just carried on saving five or ten pounds at a time, because I'd got into the habit.

I sometimes think that I know Roza's stories better than I know my own. My background was modest and sane, and there was plenty of love simmering away serenely under all the polite English restraint. I had a friend in the late fifties who used to play comic songs on the piano, and every now and then he'd stop dead in the middle of a number and sing, 'Thank God I'm normal.' He always stopped and inserted 'Have a banana' at some point as well. Anyway, my family was quite normal, and I've always been normal, sad to say. It didn't leave me with many stories. It was all so normal that I didn't know whether to thank God or curse Him.

8
Apple

Dreams are the same always.

I came by on the day that Airey Neave was killed by the IRA, and found Roza in a penitent mood because she had been horrible to the Bob Dylan upstairs. She was consoling herself with a bottle of white wine from the fridge, and she offered me some, so I said, 'I'd love one, but don't ever let me drink more than a glass and a half!'

'Why not? It's good for you. Without wine there is no civilisation,' said Roza, and I replied, 'Well, it isn't good for me. It makes me go very strange. I've almost had to stop, so a glass and a half's my limit.'

'Ooh, what does it do to you?' she asked, her eyes bright with a sort of delighted curiosity.

'Do you know that story about Jekyll and Hyde?'

'Who?'

'Jekyll and Hyde. I don't suppose there's any reason why you would have heard of it. It's about a doctor who takes a potion and it turns him into a murderer until the potion wears off. Well, that's what happens with alcohol and me, except that it's me who usually ends up nearly being murdered. I suddenly get in a terrible rage, and more often than not I get in a fight.

Afterwards I often don't really know why it all happened. The last time, I picked a fight with a damn great Irish hod carrier in a pub in Watford, and it was a very bad idea, I can tell you. I miss not being able to drink, but really I've got no choice. I have to watch what I do. I haven't made an idiot of myself for about ten years now, thank God.'

'You get in fights? I can't imagine you in fights, Chris. You always seem so sweet and nice.'

'Well, I am nice until I've had too much. Just give me half a glass, I'll be happy with that, and there won't be any danger. So, what was this quarrel with the Bob Dylan about?'

Apparently he had brought in a young cat, having offered to look after it for someone, and she had thrown a fit and started shouting at him to get rid of it. He must have been made of sterner stuff than me, because he told her to get lost, and took the cat upstairs to his room. He probably hadn't heard about the filleting knife in her handbag yet.

She said she had a phobia about cats, but she hadn't meant to shout and scream at the Bob Dylan, because the Bob Dylan was very nice and would listen to her poetry. 'Poetry?' I said. 'What poetry? I didn't know you wrote poetry.'

She said, 'I didn't tell you. You're not a poem type.'

I was offended by this aspersion of philistinism, but actually she was right. Until I got to know Roza I never did give a damn about poetry. I couldn't see what it was for. It was never anywhere inside my horizon. I once asked the Bob Dylan what Roza's poetry was like, and he said, 'It's in Serbo-Croat, so I don't really know, but when she translates it into English it's like Chinese poetry.'

I wasn't enlightened, so the Bob Dylan said, 'It consists of strings of apparently disconnected observations linked together by the last line, which is a kind of comment.'

Talking to the Bob Dylan made me realise that there was an awful lot I didn't know, and it was embarrassing that he was giving me information when he was only half my age, but then the general trouble with ignorance is always that the ignorant person has no idea that that's what they are. You can be ignorant and stupid and go through your whole life without ever encountering any evidence against the hypothesis that you're a genius. If you're stupid you can always blame miscalculation on bad luck. Anyway, the fact that Roza wrote poetry raised her further in my estimation, even though I didn't care about poetry itself. I just knew that one was supposed to. I liked reading western novels, people like Louis L'Amour, that was my idea of a good read. Roza made a big difference, she did make me improve my quality control, and I do enjoy reading a little poetry these days, but now that I am an oldish man, it's probably too late to develop decent literary tastes, although my daughter is still doing her best to educate me. She wants me to read *Middlemarch*, but it's so damned big that I just don't have the heart. She sent it to me for Christmas, all the way from New Zealand.

I hadn't expected that a prostitute would be a writer of poetry. You don't think of them as proper people. You don't think of them as someone who might shop in a supermarket or go for a swim. Roza always surprised me by being a human being, just as I surprised myself by getting so enmeshed with her. It was stupid of me not to realise that prostitutes go to movies, and walk in the park like anyone else. We all deceive ourselves with simplifications, and so you can't imagine a prostitute going shopping any more than you can imagine a soldier being interested in lepidoptery, or a monarch sitting on the loo.

Roza always said that she'd been happy as a child, and there wasn't much that bothered her about her memories, apart from finding a corpse in a hayrick, and the occasion when her father struck her mother.

'It was good to be a solitary child in that criss-cross of wheatfields and ditches. I was solitary because my brother Friedrich was born in 1946. They gave him that name in honour of Engels. I waited until 1960. My mother said I was a nice accident, but for all I know it was because of a night when my father made her do it and she never got round to getting rid of me in time.'

Her brother Friedrich used to come home with his friends and tease her by saying things like 'What's a titty, Roza? How many tits does a girl have?' and she would guess and say, 'Three or four,' thereby providing the boys with some congenial hilarity. When they laughed they used to pummel each other. Friedrich used to apologise afterwards for teasing her, but he didn't stop. Later on he became an officer in the federal army, and she saw very little of him after that.

Roza was named after Rosa Luxemburg, even though the latter was very ugly and came to a nasty end. She was a communist heroine, or so Roza told me, but I can't now remember what it was that she was supposed to have done. I saw a photograph of my Roza as a child, and she was far from ugly. She looked sturdy, but pretty and sweet. When I looked at the picture I got a pang of regret in my stomach for what Roza had turned into, but that didn't stop me from fantasising about her.

Roza had gypsy eyes, her hair was very black and shiny, and parted down the middle. She had a soft full mouth, and it looked to me as if her complexion had been pretty good until she had started to overdo the alcohol and cigarettes. She told me that she used to look at herself in a mirror and do pirouettes, and wonder if she'd ever be beautiful enough to be carried away by a prince. I said, 'That doesn't sound like a very communist line of thinking,' and she just shrugged and said, 'Dreams are the same always.'

Even when I knew her, Roza was somewhat obsessed with counting things, but she was a lot worse as a child, apparently. She'd count her fingers even though she knew she hadn't lost one, and as she counted them she folded them back to make sure that she hadn't counted a finger twice. When we went for walks she would count railings, or the number of people with hats on. She was distressed by falling snow, because snowflakes were innumerable. She had a philosophy of numbers. One was the number of her father's eyes, two was the number of her own, and the number of his gold teeth. Three was the number of swings of the starting handle that it took to start her father's car, and four was the number of its wheels. Five was the number of fingers on one hand, and six was the age when she got her first pocket money. And so it went on. She hated the number seven because there wasn't anything it could stand for. I once tried to tease her clumsily by saying,

'So what's special about five hundred?' and she looked at me with disdain, dropped some ash into the ashtray, looked away, and said, 'It's what I said I used to fuck for.'

I said, 'And what do you do it for now?' I said it lightly, as if I were joking, but she replied, 'Why are you saying this?' so I fell silent. I felt hot with embarrassment and was thinking that I had made a terrible mistake, but then the Bob Dylan upstairs came in and told us his latest stupid joke, so the situation was saved.

Roza didn't have an imaginary friend. I didn't either, come to that. She used to talk about all the characters in the folk tales that her grandmother told her. This grandmother was bald and used to hide it by wearing a shawl. She wore widow's black, and had the kind of shoes that you can put on either foot, to save trouble. I have never come across this kind of shoe in my life and now I wonder if Roza was making it up. The grandmother, according to Roza, had a great hairy wart on her right cheek, so that to kiss her cheek was like kissing a man's. She told stories about a great-uncle who won a fight with a bear, and about her own grandmother's sister who escaped from a tyrannical husband by crossing the Dinaric Alps in the company of some brigands. Then she sailed to Cephalonia on a fishing boat, and set up house with a man called Gerasimos. Years later she came back with two grown-up sons as big as houses, in order to demand a divorce. It seems that she wanted to legitimise the boys and make Gerasimos an honest man before he went to his grave.

I liked Roza's stories, but now I am confused as to which ones were supposed to be historically factual.

There was someone called 'Black George', I remember, and someone called Matija Gubec. She knew very bloodthirsty stories, always about Turks, which she told with great relish and some show of righteous horror. One story was about an emperor who blinded all his prisoners except for one in every hundred, who was supposed to lead the others home, and when the opposing king saw what had happened to his troops, he died of the shock. Then there was the story about Prince Michael's tragic love affair, and another one about how Gubec was taken to Zagreb cathedral and crowned 'King of the Peasants' by having a white-hot circle of iron placed on his head while the crowd stood there cheering and waving their hats. Roza often got angry when telling these stories, and they explain why she hated so many different peoples, Turks, Croats, Albanians, just about everyone else in the region. I once heard a joke about Irish Alzheimer's disease, which is when you forget everything but a grudge, and if Roza was anything to go by, I would say that that would be a pretty good description of Balkan Alzheimer's too. I tried telling her all the favourite British national myths, like King Alfred and the cakes, and Robert the Bruce and the spider, but somehow they never quite matched up to stories about people being crowned with white-hot circles of steel. Many years later my daughter told me that King Edward II had been killed by having a white-hot poker pushed up his backside, and I thought that that was exactly the kind of story that Roza might have appreciated. I felt sorry that she wasn't there for me to tell her.

Roza was able to make friends with wild animals.

She said she'd go out into the sunflower fields and flatten herself a little space that could only be seen by birds, and then she'd sit so still that the animals would start to get used to her. She laughed at herself when she told me this, but she said that she would think of mice as her messengers, and she thought of rabbits as lords and ladies. Beetles were Russian spies or Turkish assassins, if I remember rightly, and foxes were princes and princesses. Roza herself had a fantasy about being a princess, and she was uncommonly obsessed with royalty for someone who said she was a communist. I knew her before the days of Princess Diana, but I've no doubt that she must have enjoyed that phenomenon while it lasted. I remember having to have conversations with her about Princess Margaret and Group Captain Peter Townsend, and the Duke of Windsor and Mrs Simpson, and finding that she knew much more about them than I did.

Roza said she'd get very brown in the summer, and her hair would lighten to a dark reddish brown. I could see it when we went for walks in the summer. She liked walks. She said that if she ever left London the thing she would miss most would be the parks with their gaggles of ducks being fed by old ladies. I once said to her, 'If rabbits are lords and ladies, what are ducks?' and she said, 'They are the stupid ones who tell the king how great he is,' and I said, 'Oh, you mean courtiers.'

In the winters of her childhood Roza would be wrapped up and sent out to get some colour into her cheeks. In hard winters the snow was six feet deep, or even deeper where the wind had drifted it, so you could jump up and down on it and then disappear when it gave way. Roza was fond of sitting in front of the fire with her feet in a bowl of hot water as she thawed out, feeling hot and cold at the same time. I liked her description of doing that, because it was just like my memory of staying in Shropshire with my grandparents, where it was so cold at Christmas that there'd be frost on the inside of the windowpanes in the mornings, and you wore jumpers and a woolly hat and socks in bed. When it snowed and gathered into drifts, you could cut tunnels into them and make little dens. One collapsed on me once, and I suppose I was lucky to get out, but in those days we were a lot less precious about children taking risks. My mother used to say, 'Go out and play, and don't come back till it's dark.' We'd stay in the woods all day, making dens, climbing trees and trying to dam streams. My brother and sisters and I made an igloo once with the help of our mother. People always said that Eskimos were very warm inside them, but we were bloody freezing. The snow wasn't right for the job, either. When you cut it into bricks it fell apart, so we made our igloo by whacking the snow with a shovel to pack it tight. When we were building it I thought I'd never seen my mother looking so young and happy. Her cheeks went red as apples, and her breath was sending puffs of vapour into the air, and when it was finished we went inside and she made a pot of tea. We sat in there shivering and drinking tea until we couldn't bear it any more. I've never had tea that tasted hotter and sweeter. I hope that my daughter has memories of me as sweet as the ones I have of my mother. Roza said that the partisans in the war sometimes made ice houses in the forest, and you could mould little shelves inside them out of the snow, and you'd hang a canvas flap over the entrance, and use kerosene lamps for light. All I can say is, I'm glad that someone did it, and that it wasn't me. I'm probably like any other travelling salesman; I regret my lack of natural heroism and adventurousness, but in the final analysis I'm damned if I want to do anything about it. I wouldn't want to be a partisan unless I got week-ends off and all missions were optional.

I realise I have digressed rather a lot from the story of the Bob Dylan upstairs and Roza's cat phobia, but I am getting there eventually. She assured me that she was truly an animal lover, the sort of person who feeds apples to horses and throws sticks for other people's dogs. In fact she used to do that when we were in parks, so I know that's true.

What happened was that one day her father came home with a muddy canvas bag in his hand, and said, 'Look what I found.' He put it on the table, and they all looked inside, and there was a ragged little kitten whose eyes were barely open. Her father had heard it mewing by the river. Someone had tied up the neck of the bag, and thrown it in, and it had floated down the river and caught on something at the bankside. He'd hooked it out with a stick.

Roza's mother said, 'It won't live. You should have finished it off.'

He said, 'What do you think, Printzeza?' and Roza had touched it with the tip of her finger and said, 'I want it.'

He said, 'Will you be upset if it dies?' and she said, 'Yes,' so he answered, 'You'd better look after it well, then.'

The kitten grew up at first with a litter of rabbits,

because rabbits allegedly can't count, and a mother rabbit doesn't mind if one of her babies doesn't look quite like the others. Oddly enough, I have heard of rabbit kittens being brought up by a cat whose real kittens have been drowned.

Anyway, the kitten suckled alongside the little rabbits, pumping away with its paws, and purring no doubt, until it was old enough to abandon rabbithood and become a cat. Roza carried it around inside her shirt, and called it Apple. She said that it tried to suckle at her nipple, and it was a delicious but alarming feeling. I felt a mild sense of injustice because I had never been invited anywhere near her nipple.

I get tired of people telling me how wonderful their pets are. Somehow I do believe that my own dog or cat is truly exceptional and marvellous, but I become impatient and sceptical when I hear it of other people's. I had to listen to Roza telling me about how sweet Apple was, how she would press her ear to the cat's flanks to listen to its heart, or let it under the blankets at night, so that it would suck at her nightdress, and how the cat never quite gave up being a rabbit, and would perch on top of the rabbit hutch, and how it was a retrieving cat, and she would roll paper into a ball and flick it across the room, and the cat would go and fetch it and bring it back and put it into a shoe so that she had to dig it out before she could throw it again. Roza's favourite story about it was that once she had placed some gristle in the cat's bowl, and the cat had picked it out and left it in her shoe, so that it had squished against her foot when she'd put the shoe on in the morning.

The cat came to a gruesome end because Roza's grandmother gave her a pet linnet. I believe it's still quite common in that part of the world to keep wild birds as pets. I had a raffish magpie when I was a child, but I don't think anyone would keep ordinary British songbirds these days.

Roza was as romantic about the linnet as I might have expected. I listened to how the bird had a handsome red breast, and red splashes on its forehead. When it was discontented it would call, 'Soo-eet, soo-eet.' When it flew about the house it dropped guano on everything indiscriminately, which is what all birds do without exception, as far as I know. It must be nice to be shamelessly incontinent without having to suffer the consequences.

In spring the bird tried to mate with Roza. It drooped its wings, spread its tail and shook its feathers. It turned in little circles and called in low sweet notes, and then it hopped onto her finger and beat its wings, and lo and behold, it would leave a drop of milt on her finger. I felt that sense of injustice again, every time she reminisced about it.

Well, I almost knew in advance what Roza was going to say next. If you have a linnet flying about the house, and a cat sleeping on a windowsill, and the linnet flies into the window and drops on the sill, you can't blame the cat for what happens next. Roza said that she was only a little girl at the time, and didn't really understand about the icy indifference of nature.

Apple ran under a chair with the bird flapping in her jaws, and Roza screamed and tried to take it from her. The cat retreated further under the chair, and Roza tried to pull the bird away from her, only to find that she now had its headless body in her hand. Apple slashed at her arm and left on it a row of stinging parallel cuts, and then went into a proper attack, biting into her arm and raking it with her hind claws.

Roza started screaming, and tried to shake the enraged cat off. I didn't quite get the details, but I think that Roza shook her arm too violently, and the cat went flying across the room, with the consequence that she ended up with two dead pets.

Her father came in and tried to console her. She said that he smelled of tobacco and eau de cologne and that it was very comforting. They collected up the two bits of the bird first, and its eyes were still bright, which upset her a lot, but that didn't upset her as much as finding that the cat had broken its neck.

Most people have had beloved pets die suddenly, so anyone can imagine what Roza felt, bearing in mind that she was only a little girl at the time. She thought she was a murderer and got frightened that she was going to be put in prison.

She buried the cat and the bird side by side at the end of the garden, and then she was sent away to stay with her bald grandmother for a couple of days. Unfortunately, when she got back she went straight to the grave and found that she hadn't dug it deep enough. The linnet had gone completely, and the cat had had its stomach eaten out. The cavity was dark red and jagged, and the stink was awful because it was summer. The maggots had already got busy too, especially at the mouth and back end, so it looked as if her teeth were in motion. She reburied it as deep as she could dig, and afterwards never could face having another cat.

When Roza told me this story, she concluded by saying that she was horrified by cats because she was frightened that she would hurt them, and that's why she'd wanted the Bob Dylan upstairs to keep the cat confined to his room.

I did my best to listen carefully and to express my sympathy, but to be honest I was more overtaken by the violent curiosity to know about her life as a prostitute. I was a prurient voyeur, I suppose.

As she got fonder of me she'd give me a little hug at the door when I left, and a kiss on each cheek, French-style. Once she let her hand rest on my arm, and she said, 'I like you because you listen to me. You make me feel that I'm interesting.'

I said, 'I've never met anyone more interesting,' and she kissed me again.

9
Survivor of Jasenovac

I couldn't stay away from Roza, not that I tried very hard.

I couldn't stay away from Roza, not that I tried very hard. I'm one of those people who's like a cat, who only feels guilty if it gets caught, and in any case it was so easy to stop off on my way home from my journeys, or even make a detour to call in on her. There were three practices in the vicinity, and I was covering a huge area of southern England, so I had no regular hours anyway. Sometimes I'd phone to make sure she was there and was feeling sociable, so I often spoke to the Jewish actor, who was the only one there with a telephone. He didn't seem to mind being my messenger, and Roza hardly ever told me not to come. When I arrived she used to kiss me on both cheeks, which I enjoyed even though it wasn't very British behaviour back in those days. Of course everyone's gone Continental now, and you even kiss your mortal enemy.

Roza would make strong black coffee on that appallingly filthy stove, and off we'd go to the living room and sit either side of the gas fire while she smoked and told me more stories about her life. It amazes me now that I sat so patiently and listened to it all, but in fact I was just as interested in the stories as I was in Roza herself. I felt I was learning a great deal. I'm surprised that my wife never noticed that I smelled of cigarette smoke when I came home, but in truth she had stopped noticing me at all many years before. She spent my money, but apart from that she had no interest in anything I said or did, and it never mattered how generous I was, I was still just a ghost in my own house.

I am glad to say that I never did smoke; I tried it at the age of twelve, and I vomited. I've known so many people die of it, in so many horrible ways, that if I was a dictator I'd round up everyone involved in the trade, charge them with mass murder, and have them shot.

It would have turned out better if I hadn't become so crazy about Roza. If I wasn't in love, I wonder how else you would have described it. I don't have any understanding of what being in love is, though I think it's happened to me a few times, and especially with Roza. You can't look it up in medical encyclopedias, and you don't get documentaries about it on the television. I have been thinking recently that it's learned from films and novels and songs, and there's probably nothing natural about it. How do you disentangle love from lust? At least lust is comprehensible. Perhaps love is the torment that damned-up lust unleashes against you.

I don't have the confidence to know what the right word is, but I was certainly entranced. Perhaps it was to do with her having been a prostitute. In my little world, that was fantastically exotic. It was like being friends with a cobra or a cougar. I admired myself for my daring. I thought I was somewhere out on the far side.

The odd thing is that I've become her surrogate, and now it's me who relates her tales. I have become a virtuoso Roza substitute. I have a compulsion to tell people everything I know about her, as if it were important to anyone but me. I even know her house near Belgrade as if I had lived there myself. I haven't been there, but I retain Roza's memories as if they were my own.

It was two kilometres outside the nearest village, and was originally very shabby, with only undercoat on the window frames, and unpainted lime-mortar walls. They had long fissures in them, one so wide that it had owls living in it until it was patched up. The roof had heavy red tiles, and it was so distorted by age that for a long time there had to be buckets placed at various strategic points. It was one of those places where in the old days people would have kept animals on the ground floor in order to warm the humans on the floor above. In Roza's time, downstairs was where the kitchen was, and there were two rooms that an estate agent would describe as 'reception' areas, but which weren't used much because the family mainly inhabited the kitchen. It had flagstones that were strewn with matting, and Roza used to express retrospective exasperation with how often she used to trip on their upturned corners.

Upstairs were three little bedrooms and a creaky landing, whose walls were decorated with the portraits of old partisan comrades, all of them very young and thin and apparently without a care, posing alongside Italian tanks, or sitting in a row on the barrel of a field gun. There was a picture of Marshall Tito shaking hands with Roza's father, and a picture of Winston Churchill waving a cigar. There was one of Stalin, and one of

Fidel Castro with his own huge Havana and prophetic beard. These four men were her father's heroes.

Roza says that she didn't like to throw anything away, so her room was a complete mess. She collected clockwork toys, dolls, and things like slide rules. She says that she had *Das Kapital* on her bookshelf, alongside the works of Shakespeare, books about folklore, and pre-communist children's books detailing the activities and adventures of various rabbits and kittens who dressed in human clothes and carried loaves of bread around in baskets. There was a row of machine-gun bullet holes stitched diagonally across the wall, left over from the Battle of Belgrade, and there was an Ottoman musket ball embedded in the woodwork of the windowsill.

Roza was fond of remembering her bed, and often wished that she had it with her in London. It was well moulded to her body, she said, and excellent for prolonged hibernation, surreptitious naps and general escapes. She would go to sleep at night with the dim light filtering up from downstairs through the interstices of the floorboards, and the frightening shrieks and whoops of owls and foxes coming in from outside. The bedhead had brass bars that you could tap with a fork or a pen, and play parts of melodies out of tune.

Roza's bedroom in that shambolic house in Archway was quite a contrast. She'd done the best she could, given that the plaster was falling off the walls and the wiring was draped about in festoons. What I remember most is that almost everything was dark pink. Perhaps 'puce' is the best word. She'd found a puce carpet, a puce coverlet for the bed, puce curtains and puce cushions. It was either very bold or in very bad taste, depending on your inclination. I imagine that people like Barbara Cartland would have had decor very similar to that. It gave me the impression of exaggerated and oppressive femininity, especially when you took into account the heavy smell of perfumes and soaps and lotions. Maybe it was just the ambience of whores.

The most amazing thing about her bedroom was that she'd stacked the legs of the bed up on bricks so that she could put a large trunk underneath it. She told me that this trunk contained all the cash earnings from her years on the game, that it was completely full, and now that she'd retired, she was going to live off it for as long as she could, preferably forever.

I was shocked and angry that she'd let me know, because she shouldn't have told anyone at all. It exposed her to too much risk. She was very surprised when I said how foolish she was to go round telling people, and she said, 'But I'm telling only my friends.'

'You shouldn't have told me,' I said. 'I don't want that kind of temptation. I don't even trust myself that much,' and she replied, 'But I know you wouldn't steal it.'

'Of course I wouldn't. But you shouldn't trust me, nor anyone else. It's stupid!'

'Oh, sorry,' she said, but not as if she meant it. She was just trying to close the conversation.

I said, 'Think what someone might do to you if they came here and decided to rob you when you were in the house!'

'OK, I'm stupid,' she said, with equally cool insincerity. 'I do stupid things. I've done lots of stupid things. Maybe I always will.'

If Roza's bedroom in Archway was quite a contrast

with her one at home in Yugoslavia, the garden must have been even more so. In Archway there was a concrete yard laid at the level of the basement doors, which should have opened but didn't, until the Bob Dylan Upstairs managed to unstick them. There was no light in this yard, and its walls were exceedingly high on account of its having been sunk so deep. Over the years people had dumped mattresses and fridges and all sorts of rubbish over the walls. I often saw rats through what had once been the French windows. There was one skinny buddleia poking out of the brickwork halfway up the wall. It produced three token purple blossoms every summer. In years past it had probably been a very lovely courtyard indeed.

In Yugoslavia they'd had a little wilderness of poorly tended fruit trees, and long grass that was kept in check by moving the rabbit and chicken pens around. Roza told me the names of the herbs and wild flowers that grew there, but she didn't know them in English, and in any case I am not a great one for flowers. When she was talking about them, I just nodded and thought about something else. One of the very few things that my wife did was tend the garden, but I had to do all the heavy work of course. I can recognise a rose and a daffodil, and that's about it. Roza said that their garden was very beautiful. She was nostalgic about the big vegetables they used to grow, and for the sunflower seeds that you could eat like sweets. She said that English vegetables compared to Yugoslavian ones were like the balls of a little boy compared to the balls of a bull. It was an unexpectedly picturesque analogy.

They had a well in the garden that you could yell

or throw stones into. When she was small Roza thought there were serpents down there, and she had nightmares about falling into it eternally, without ever hitting the water. I used to have nightmares about having petrol poured over me, and being set on fire, and nowadays I have nightmares that I have wooden teeth and that they are continually falling out, as if I had an infinite number of them. It seems that everyone has their own inexplicable fear to have nightmares about. We need nightmares to keep ourselves entertained, and fend off the contentment that we all fear and abhor so much.

She liked the rabbits, even though the does sometimes ate their babies, and she hated the chickens because of their stupid violence, always pecking at each other's rumps and tearing each other's feathers out. She threw a dead sparrow into their pen one day, and they tore it to pieces. She maintained that chickens were like the Balkan people in general, with their constant and implacable pecking at each other's bloody backsides.

The hens were kept mainly for their eggs, and generally you ate the old cockerels unless you had visitors. Roza had a farmyard folk tale about an old cockerel that was replaced by a new one. Realising that he might soon be eaten, he challenged the young cock to a race, specifying that he wanted a start, in order to make fair allowance for his age. The young cock was agreeable, and so the older one began to run off, soon to be followed by the younger one. The farmer saw this out of the window, and the upshot was that the farmer ate the younger one, on the grounds that no one needs a homosexual rooster. I was never any good at telling jokes.

'One good thing about growing up in the country,'

said Roza one day, 'was that I learned to kill things, and it was OK. I broke the necks on rabbits.'

She looked at me with a sinister and knowing expression on her face, and I felt distinctly uneasy. I took the remark as a vaguely intended threat, especially after she told me about the knife in her bag.

For years Roza's family had an outside privy that stank in the high summer, but was otherwise a good place for contemplation and seclusion. It was a brick lean-to, much deformed by subsidence, and its seat was a thick wooden plank with an oval hole cut in it. If you shone a torch down there, you could see thousands of big white maggots, and if you dropped anything in it by accident, you just had to forget about it. It was frightening to have to go there at night, because of the scuffling and grunting of nocturnal animals. In a little girl's mind they were easily magnified into tigers and bears. Roza said that the very worst thing was having to sit there in the winter, when it felt as though the skin was going to be torn off the backs of the legs. Her brother told her that if your backside froze to the board, they'd have to cut your bum off to free you, so in winter she'd lie awake all night trying to hold it in. Funnily enough, I remember all these kinds of things from the house in Shropshire. In that place there was an outside loo with three holes cut in a row so that people could be sociable. It's probably illegal nowadays. I expect that it's been outlawed by the European Union.

Roza's father used to warm up the seat with a methylated-spirit blowtorch, and it wasn't until that packed up that he installed a proper system, with a pipe into the bottom of the well that fed a tank in the roof space, so they wouldn't have to break ice or melt snow any more. A water heater was put in, the lavatory moved indoors, and the old one was covered over to serve as a cesspit. Roza said that after all this, life lost some of the element of struggle that had made it fun. You didn't have that delicious sense of anticipation as a big cauldron of water heated up. Her father said that it was strange not having to live like a partisan any more, and complained about everyone getting soft.

They had a car that had been liberated from the Germans at the end of the war, an old Mercedes staff car with red seats that smelled wonderful and made you feel very lordly and disdainful when you drove about in it. It was powerful, but too grand to drive fast, and Roza's father used to sit at the wheel looking straight ahead while he got overtaken by Skodas and Voskhod mopeds. He used it daily to go to his offices in Belgrade, and after work he would quite often be irritated to find it surrounded by tourists posing for photographs next to it. If anything went wrong, a tremendous fuss would have to be made before spares could be found or made up, and in the meantime they would have to use public transport, which Roza alleged would always smell of goats, baby vomit and raw onions. She was like a lot of the Labour politicians we used to have in Britain back then, such as Anthony Wedgwood Benn; she was a toff who approved of the common people as long as she didn't have to mix with them.

She told me that there was an orchard nearby where she used to climb trees, and that was where she first started trying to write poems. I once sat for hours while she solemnly read her poems to me in Serbo-Croat, and then explained what they meant. It was pleasant watching her face as she read, because she was experiencing the emotions, her spirit shone out, and I liked being able to stare at her for a long time without her realising that I was admiring her. What struck me was how strange language is, when you don't know what it means. She told me that the Bob Dylan Upstairs also wrote poetry, and I thought, 'Oh dear.' Since I've known Roza I've struggled with modern poetry from time to time, but I confess that it often seems just like ordinary language cut up, or lists of cryptic crossword-puzzle clues. I need someone in the know to explain it to me. When I was at school we learned lots of poetry, but it was the dumdedum kind, with lots of rhymes, and the lines all the same length. I wasn't kitted out for the modern stuff at all. Anyway, I never did read or hear any of the BDU's poetry. He could be famous by now, for all I know.

I can understand why Roza might have wanted to spend hours up a tree, however. I did a lot of that when I was a boy. I went back recently and saw that the little tree I used to climb up has grown into a fairly large oak. I haven't felt such a pang of lost time and painful nostalgia in many a year.

Anyway, once Roza got into trouble for cutting open hundreds of apples in this orchard after her bald grandmother told her a folk tale about an apple with a diamond in it. She was made to gather up all the dismembered fruit in a wheelbarrow and take it down the road to a piggery. Roza liked the same things about her orchard as I did about the one in Shropshire. Sunlight coming through the leaves. Field mice. Sparrows mating. Starlings or fieldfares settling all around you because they hadn't noticed you. I said to Roza, 'One day I'll take you to the house in Shropshire where I spent a lot of my youth.' She was pleased by that, but in fact we never did get round to it. It's difficult to get time off with a young retired Yugoslavian prostitute when you've got a Great White Loaf at home expecting you to lay paving slabs and take your daughter to the cinema while she knits. Everything that happened with Roza and me occurred in that derelict and filthy house in Archway, mostly in the basement, always before I went home to Limbo in glamorous Sutton.

One day Roza had an experience that she found very shocking, and it was brought about by a horse.

She was picking up windfalls when she felt a nudging at her shoulder, and then a tugging at her jumper. She cried out with shock, and the equally startled horse shied and cantered away, kicking up its hind legs and whinnying. It was a very big carthorse, and it had a mouthful of red wool that it had detached from Roza's jumper.

She decided to run away, but a peasant woman turned up at the gate, huffing and puffing, and wanting to know if she had seen a horse, which was quite conspicuously nearby, eating apples.

The upshot of all this was that the hairy-faced old lady offered Roza a ride on the horse, and she was too terrified to refuse. It was difficult to mount such a big horse, and it had to be done by climbing on a gate first, but she was determined not to panic, and she stayed up there by clutching on to the mane. She thought it was trying to bite her feet, but the old lady said that it was just sniffing her to see who she was.

Off they went along the road, with the horse farting on account of the apples, which made Roza giggle, but did not impress the old lady, and they had gone quite a way before she said that she thought that this was probably far enough, otherwise it would take too long for Roza to get home, and anyway, it was about to rain.

Roza didn't want to go, and she made the woman promise to let her ride the horse again. It was apparently called 'Russia' because it was very big, a complete liability, and always going where it wasn't wanted. She sprained her ankle getting off, and after the tears were duly wiped, she started to limp home.

She was only halfway there when the wellhead broke with a clap of thunder, and down fell the rain. Her ankle hurt too much to run, and the water was beginning to fall very heavily, so she made for a little barn that was at the side of the road. It was heaped with bales of straw, and she climbed up on them despite being frightened of rats.

She said that she mostly felt very disappointed about having to get off the horse, and annoyed about being caught in the rain, and at first was more puzzled than alarmed by catching sight of a hand sticking up out of the straw. It was like a yellow claw, with papery skin.

She moved some straw away, and the long and short of it is that she found a dead tramp. Fortunately she thought he was asleep, and her first instinct was not to wake him up, as that would have been bad manners. He was wearing a placard around his neck, on which was scrawled: '*Survivor of Jasenovac. Hero of the Resistance.*' He had a medal with a red ribbon pinned to his chest, his mouth was open and his lips were blue. He had a white beard, speckled with vomit. Next to him was a brown bottle, which later turned out to have had carbon tetrachloride industrial dry-cleaner in it. Roza said that when she sniffed at the empty bottle she thought it smelled very nice. Luckily it was all gone, so she didn't get to take a swig of it.

She tried conversing with him, but did eventually realise that he was dead. At that point she went out in the rain and limped home, regardless.

Her parents were furious with her, mostly because of their own anxiety. They were in their coats and hats and were just about to set out looking for her. It was particularly bad for her father because thunder made him feel as if he were back under bombardment. It took her a little while to persuade them that there really was a dead man in the barn down the road, and they accused her of telling tales and told her to stop telling lies. What ultimately persuaded them was her odd assertion that the dead man's name was 'Survivor of Jasenovac', since she couldn't possibly have thought that one up on her own.

When the police took away the body, they finally identified it as being indeed that of a beggar and one-time resistance fighter, who had been captured and put into the extermination camp at Jasenovac. I looked it up and discovered that this was a place where the Croats had killed about thirty-five thousand Serbs. The Gestapo had inspected it and been shocked. Some of the staff were Franciscan monks. When Yugoslavia finally fell apart, I was one of those people who wasn't particularly surprised. Roza always said that it would, after Tito died. I didn't believe her at first, though; we'd all been told that it was a multicultural paradise, positively purulent with harmony and sweet understanding.

Roza said that the reason she still got upset about the tramp was that you could be a hero and survive in hell, and get awarded the Partisan Star, and then still die like a rat, and it's just another day, and nothing's changed. Roza said that the episode gave her horrible feelings about the futility of life's struggles. I remember another time when she said that if you felt that life was futile, it had a liberating effect, because then you were prepared to do almost anything. I remember talking to a philosopher in a bar once. He was another one who was delaying going home to his wife. He advised me that I should never be frightened of failure, because one day I was going to die anyway.

I told her, 'I found a dead man once. It was under an archway in King's Cross.' I don't know why I told Roza that. It wasn't even true. I don't often tell lies on impulse. There was a song that all the kids with guitars were singing at the time, and one of the verses was about 'one more forgotten hero, and a world that doesn't care'. It was called 'The Streets of London', or something, and it was all about derelict old people. I must have got the idea from that.

She exhaled some smoke and said, 'I saw another dead man. He was only just dead.'

I didn't ask her to explain. Just then I had to get home to Sutton. It was my wife's birthday, I hadn't yet finished my rounds, and I was running out of reasonable excuses. I only remembered her remark later. When Roza said goodnight at the door she put her hands on my shoulders and briefly laid her head on my chest. I thought, 'I'm making progress,' and I went away feeling pleased with myself. I'd saved about a hundred pounds by then, and was still wondering what to do with it. I was feeling disgusted and irritated with myself that I had ever thought of offering it to Roza.

10
Miss Radic

Beware of getting a disengaged heart.

I had an embarrassing encounter in the local library. It was a little dingy place, which is how I like libraries to be. I'd gone in to read up about Yugoslavia, and I found a book called *A Concise History of the Yugoslav Peoples*. I was going to read it in the library, because I wasn't a member yet, and couldn't take it away. I had a notebook with me so that I could record the more interesting details and memorise them.

The newspapers were full of stuff about the Yorkshire Ripper, but I was sitting at a table reading about the Battle of Kosovo.

Someone tapped me on the shoulder. When I looked up, I saw it was Chris, and my face started to burn. I was so confused and embarrassed. He kissed me on the cheek. 'Hi,' he said. 'I called round at your place, but you weren't there, so I thought I'd come here and while away the time. I thought I'd pop in and see if they'd got anything on Yugoslavia.' He leaned over and looked at my book, and said, 'I see that you've got just the thing.'

I was expecting him to ask me awkward questions as to why I was reading about my own country, but he didn't. It probably didn't strike him as strange at all. I suppose that lots of people read histories of their own countries. It was just me feeling as though I'd been caught out, looking for stories. It also seemed strange to come across him out of context, like meeting one of your teachers in the street at a weekend.

'I'd better let you finish it first,' he said. 'I can always order it from the library in Sutton.'

I said, 'Well, let's go back to my place, now that we've met up.' We went for a stroll first, and watched old ladies feeding birds. He said, 'Have you ever noticed how many city pigeons have only got one foot, or have a foot that's mangled?'

I said that I hadn't, but from that day to this I've noticed it a lot.

I used to enjoy teasing Chris by being very frank. I think he was often appalled. I was testing him, to see how far I could go. I wonder if he was ever puzzled about why I told him personal things in such detail, things that normal people would keep to themselves, or that girls would only tell to their best friend or their sister. More often than not I'd mix up these revelations with the sort of information that people bore you with at parties.

Once I told him about my favourite teacher, who was called Miss Radic.

I was the kind of pupil who always knows everything already, so I got easily bored in class. I could read before I even went to school, and was always putting my hand up and going 'Me, Miss! Me, Miss!' every time the teacher asked the class a question, and when I got told off for overeagerness I'd go on strike and cross my arms and sulk, and then the teachers would tease me and say, 'What? Don't you know the answer, Roza?'

I mostly enjoyed school. It was nice being delivered there in the big Mercedes when not many other people had cars at all. My father used to make me empty out my pencil case every morning before we went, to make sure that I had the full complement of pencils and things. He used to say, 'The more you work now, the less you'll have to work later.'

At school I got thrown in the prickly hedge, and people took rubber bands and fired folded paper in class, and there was a fashion for punching people in the upper arm to see if a big bruised area could be created. Once there was a spastic boy who was so cruelly teased and persecuted that he took to injuring himself so that he wouldn't have to go to school. Chris said to me that it sounded as if my communist Yugoslavian education had been exactly the same as his capitalist English one.

'What are those things that you make points on pencils with?' I asked him once, because my English had some gaps in it. I didn't learn it in the usual way.

'A pencil sharpener?'

'Yes, OK, pencil sharpener. I stole one from my friend at school.'

'Did you?'

'It was very pretty. It was wood, and it had a little painting on it, and so I stole it.'

'Yes?'

'And I never did use it because I felt too much shame about myself.'

'You gave it back, I suppose?'

I thought I'd tease him a bit and so I looked at him as if he were mad, and said, 'No, of course not. I've still got it. I'll show you one day.'

'And you've still never used it?'

I shook my head, and blew out smoke. I thought, 'I wonder what he'll make of that,' but he didn't say anything. Chris often didn't comment about what I said, because he was worried about making the right impression.

'I like you,' I said, 'because you listen. I tell you anything, but you don't get shocked, you just listen.'

'I do get shocked,' he admitted, 'a bit.'

'Oh, it's being polite, is it? You don't let me see, about how shocked you are? In my country everyone says that the English are hypocrites, because they're always pretending, but I think it's because the manners are too good.'

'Well, it's very interesting, listening to you. I don't want you to stop, so I don't look shocked, even if I am. These days I feel like an old man. Nobody's interested in someone like me. Youngsters look at me and I know they're thinking that I'm a retarded dinosaur with one foot in the grave. The thing about being me and being forty is that I feel I've got to offer something extra, because no one would be interested in me otherwise. Probably I'm just being stupid. The world's gone beyond my opinions, if you know what I mean. I feel old-fashioned when I get shocked, and I don't like it.'

'OK,' I said, 'I'll tell you something. When I got my first hair . . . down there . . . I didn't realise it was mine, and I pulled at it, and I only realised it was mine when it hurt.'

He definitely was shocked. 'Why did you tell me that?'

'Are you shocked?'

He reflected a moment, and denied it. 'No, not really, I've got used to you trying to shock me. The most surprising thing was when you said something about sleeping with your father.'

'I'll tell you more about that one day, if you like. Would you like it?' I leaned forward and smiled in a way that was suggestive. He looked a little angry. 'I can't help feeling that you're playing games with me. You tease me. You know, sometimes, Roza, I wonder what's going on. Sometimes I feel like the idiot in a spy book.'

I was alarmed. I didn't want him to be angry and give me up. I didn't know what to say. In the end I just got up and went and poured myself more coffee. When I came back I put my hand on his arm and said, 'Sorry.' I could feel his pleasure at being touched by me, and he smiled up at me a little weakly, and said, 'Oh, it's nothing. Really, it's me who's sorry.'

I said, 'Please don't give up on me, I couldn't bear it.'

'Why would I do that?'

'People do, sometimes.'

He looked at me and I was sure that he was in love with me. He said, 'I don't think I could ever give up on you.' I kissed him on the forehead, like a daughter. It's nice to have someone you can be affectionate with, and you know they're not dangerous. I was getting feelings too. I could sense them bubbling up. I kept wondering what it would be like if we were lovers, and whether I'd be jealous of his wife. I thought I probably wouldn't. You don't get jealous of the zookeeper who keeps the monkey in the cage. If I were going to be jealous of her, I would have started already.

'I was going to tell you about Miss Radic,' I said.

'Oh yes?'

'She was a great teacher. She told me all about women's things, having periods and getting breasts and that kind of thing. If she hadn't, I think I wouldn't have known anything.'

'My teachers were all paedophiles, sadists and megalomaniacs,' said Chris. 'I had a wonderful education, though. I can count to a hundred in Latin. I had a teacher who'd been in Africa, and now there's nothing I don't know about Zulus. He started every geography and history lesson with "When I was out in Africa . . ."'

'Did anyone teach you about being a man, you know . . . men's things?'

'Not really. When we left school the headmaster advised us that if anyone should try to interfere with us, we should kick him in the balls. If he'd told us that before, there would have been a couple of masters with aching groins. As for the facts of life, I learned most of the basics the moment I went to school, from the other boys.'

'Oh,' I said, 'I didn't have any pervert teachers. Miss Radic was nice. My mother wasn't much good, though. When I had my period she just got worried about the sheets. Miss Radic patted me on the head and said congratulations. And she told me not to get a disengaged heart.'

'A disengaged heart? What's that supposed to mean?'

'It's about sex and love,' I said. 'She meant I should keep them together.'

'And did you?'

I felt some pain inside, and said honestly, 'No, I didn't keep them together. I never did anything right.' I laughed and shook my head. 'I've been crap.' I stopped and lit another cigarette, and then I said, 'When Miss Radic told me about the facts, I cried, and I said, "I don't want to have one of those things put inside me and get pregnant." Miss Radic laughed and hugged me to her chest. She had her spectacles on a cord round her neck, and I felt them pressing into me, all hard and strange.'

Chris said, 'It's funny what memories we choose to keep.'

11

The Betrayal

I was like a fifteen-year old.

By this time I was beginning to have some problems. I was losing sleep because I just lay in my sheets sweating and itching and thinking about Roza, mentally taking her clothes off, and visualising all the things I wanted to do with her.

I was like a fifteen-year old, getting one erection after another. Even if I crept downstairs to the living room and did something about it in the dark, I'd be back in bed for only half an hour before it happened all over again, and I'd have to go back down. It became painful, and I felt I was humiliating myself, but at the same time I was amazed and proud that I had such potency left at my age, after so many years of a dry marriage and its dismal abstinence. Sometimes it was so bad that I had to take three shots of whisky before I could get myself off to sleep.

The next time I called, the door was answered by the Bob Dylan Upstairs. He looked as if he'd been crying, and he was wearing a black armband on his left arm. He was wearing the huge pair of moccasins, much too big for him, and I don't think I have ever seen anyone looking so despondent. I said, 'Oh, I'm so sorry.'

He said, 'What for?' and I said, 'Your bereavement, obviously.' I gestured towards the black armband.

'Oh,' he said, glancing down at it, 'no one's died. It's Dylan.'

'Dylan?'

'Mmm, Dylan. He's gone and cut a religious record.' His eyes filled with tears.

'Lots of people do religious records. I'm sure Cliff Richard must have done one, and my wife has several Christmas ones by people like Bing Crosby.'

He looked at me scornfully and said, 'Shit, when Dylan does it, you know it's the end. And Knopfler's playing guitar on it. You'd think that Knopfler might have tried to stop him.'

I had no idea who this Knopfler was, and had to find out from my daughter when I got home. I said to the BDU, 'Is the music no good then?'

'The music's good, but I can't take all that paranoid Christian stuff. It's all hellfire and eternal punishment and the end of the world. Jesus, Dylan used to be intelligent. He used to write about idiots who thought they had God on their side. It wouldn't be so bad, but there's no one else remotely like him. I mean, when even Dylan turns off his brain, what hope is there for the rest of us?'

I was amused. He probably felt as my father had when he'd finally realised that Oswald Mosley was a foolish peacock. I said, 'You've lost your hero, I suppose.'

'I've lost my voice. No one's speaking any more. I might as well go and work in a bank.'

I didn't quite see what was so bad about working in a bank; at least he wouldn't have had to live in a slum. But I realised that he would think less of me if I said so. Instead I said, 'That would be terrible.' But I couldn't help adding, 'You make him sound like your ventriloquist.'

He smiled and said, 'I'll have to make up my own words now. I never thought I'd have to.'

I said, 'Maybe you overestimate his importance.'

He shrugged, and I said, 'My daughter's always quoting Bob Dylan lines at me. One of her favourites is "Don't follow leaders, watch your parking meters".' The BDU looked at me in utter amazement, and I went in to see Roza feeling that I had just scored an unexpected triumph.

That morning Roza decided to tell me that when she was in her early teens she'd had a lesbian interlude. Her addiction to telling me stories never abated. As for me, I kept listening because I really was interested, and it was the one way that I could keep her enthusiastic about my coming back. It's true that I loved to watch her and fantasise about her when she was talking.

By then I'd saved up another twenty pounds. I was keeping the money in a Manila envelope in my breast pocket, because I didn't want to leave it anywhere in the house where my wife could find it. I wish now that I'd had the sense to put it in a deposit account, but I liked the feeling of being rich that having a wad of notes gives you. I had realised that saving was quite a good habit in its own right, and I was thinking that maybe when I'd reached the symbolic five hundred I should buy lots of premium bonds, and see if Ernie could make me rich.

12
Natalja

She was my ideal self.

It was such fun telling Chris my stories, even though I now wish I hadn't told him some of them. I was flattered that an older man was treating me as if I was so interesting, and anyway, I was beginning to depend on him. I could tell he was falling for me, and I knew I was falling for him. He was married, but the wife seemed theoretical to me. I'd never met her and he hardly ever mentioned her, so she didn't really exist. I started to have pretty dreams about Chris lifting me out of my life, and God knows, I could have done with being lifted out. I sometimes hoped that we could go away together and start a new life. Chris seemed to be a perfect gentleman. He was longing for me, but he never pushed himself. I used to observe the way that he looked at me when he didn't know that I was observing him. He liked to look at my breasts and my groin, and I am sure that he often leaned forward to pay attention to me because he was trying to hide whatever was happening. I liked to think about that, and it made me sweat. I was having interesting dreams about him. One of them was about taking a vase of flowers to his room, and him sitting at a desk and turning and smiling at me. That's all it was, a little dream about a simple act of love.

Anyway, my stories were the method I used to keep him coming back. Once I'd started, I couldn't stop. I couldn't have borne it if he'd lost interest. I don't know how I would have coped with the loneliness.

I knew that a lot of men were turned on by lesbians, or the thought of what they got up to anyway, so I told him the Natalja story, about when I went to a Young Communist Pioneer camp in Dalmatia.

This is what I told him:

It was the usual embarrassing stuff; folkloric dancing, community singing, long hikes, stupid games, and lectures about the heroes of communism. Even so, I liked it because the climate was nicer there, and everything smelled of seafood and lemons, and there were two little islands, and a big mountain behind us. There was something about the air that made me feel happy, I suppose. I wasn't just thinking about myself all the time, so I felt free.

One day, after we'd watched some slide shows, we went to a museum that was a Franciscan monastery, and it had the largest collection of seashells in the world. I was looking at a collection of cowries, when I smelled peaches and lavender, and I realised that it was the girl standing next to me. She said, 'I hate shells. I'd rather look at all the French boys on the beach.'

'How do you know they're French?' I asked.

'I don't. It's just that I'd like them to be. I'm Natalja, but everyone calls me Tasha. You're Roza. I asked someone.' She said, 'I think we're going to be friends.

I looked at everybody in the whole lousy camp, and you were the only one.'

I was flattered, and a bit surprised. I'd never been picked out like that before, and I didn't know how to react. She didn't seem to notice, and just carried on talking. 'You and I are the prettiest in the camp, and I thought it would be a bad idea to be enemies. Do you like boys?'

'No,' I said. 'Not yet, anyway.'

She took my arm and walked me to the next case of shells. 'I don't really, either. What I like is the idea of them. I wish I had your cheekbones. I haven't got any tits yet, but I'm still hoping.'

Tasha was taller than me, and very slender. She had the longest hair I've ever seen. It was blonde and wavy and it fell to her waist. She had to brush it aside to stop it obscuring her vision. She had dark eyebrows, and her eyes were so brown that they seemed black, and yet whenever I think of her I have to remind myself that they weren't blue.

She always wore blue, and she was usually barefoot. She liked to celebrate her willowy figure by striking melodramatic poses and declaiming lines from plays, and she could do all sorts of amazing acrobatic feats that I wouldn't have dared to try. She did cartwheels next to me when we walked, and when she did a backflip you didn't even hear her land. She was a sort of nature spirit. She once put her hands on the floor and got both feet right behind her neck. She looked at me gravely, and said, 'Do you think this position will be helpful to me when I'm married?'

I loved Tasha because she was everything that I

would have liked to have been. She was my ideal self, uninhibited, blunt, light-hearted, funny and exuberant, the sort of girl who slept unashamedly through all the slide shows and talks about communism, and scrawled her name on the monument to the Yugoslav Navy when no one was looking. She didn't want to help building a wall because she said that God had made men stupid and strong so that women didn't have to do those kinds of things. She sang out of tune and didn't care.

Tasha and I walked around the backstreets arm in arm, sucking on ice creams while she pointed out the best male backsides. They were all French, of course. We ate bowlfuls of aubergine ratatouille, dripping with olive oil, and aromatic with oregano, garlic and black pepper. Once she got up on a wall and tried to teach me how to belch at will. She lay along it like a model on a photographic shoot, rotating her hand from the wrist, with the forefinger extended, conducting her own little concert of ladylike belches. It was a way of enjoying the ratatouille all over again, she said. I was so embarrassed that I went as far away as I could without actually leaving.

She persuaded two German boys to take us to a disco, and then refused to dance with either of them. Lots of men bought us drinks, but we danced with each other, and came out at midnight with our brains reeling from the heavy bass and the flashing lights. She kissed me underneath a plane tree, and I felt my heart lurch. There was a moment when I saw the glow in her eyes, and felt her hot breath on my face, and her arms were trembling.

Tasha was a Slovene, but she lived in Belgrade because her father was a representative in the federal parliament. It was possible to continue our friendship after the camp because it was quite easy for me to get to Francuska Street. We talked on the phone so much that it irked our parents, and she often came out to stay with me in the country. My father loved her so much that it made me jealous.

Tasha was enchanting. She had a head full of dreams and fantasies that permitted her to be carried away by conquering heroes or to die of consumption in a nunnery. At one minute she was a princess, and then she was a Gypsy from Herzogovina, and then she was an Amazonian warrior, a millionairess, an actress.

I know what it was I loved in her, but I don't know what she saw in me. I was dark and stocky, a little sad and unsure, and she was the opposite. I couldn't have filled her life as she filled mine. That's the odd thing about affection, though. If you have a large amount of it to bestow, and if the right person isn't there to receive it, you bestow it on someone else until a better candidate comes along. We wrote each other letters that ended 'Your loving friend forever' or 'eternally yours', which I kept in a large brown envelope that I left under my pillow.

During our holidays we liked to go with a basket of fruit and cheese to our place by the river. There was a large shallow pool enclosed by birch trees, and sometimes you could see trout waving their tails in the current.

The first time we went there it was high summer, and Tasha wiggled her toes in the water, and found it deliciously cold. She dared me to dare her to go in, and in a trice she'd stripped and waded in. She was squealing and laughing because of the cold, and I was full of fear and admiration. She made me long for a freedom to which I wasn't psychologically suited. 'Come on in,' she called, and I shook my head. 'But it's lovely,' she said, and I was torn between my shame and my anxiety not to appear ashamed. I stripped off and waded into the water with my arms over my breasts, which were quite heavy even in those days.

I wish I could describe her body without feeling embarrassed about it. I still have the picture in my head very clearly, but you'll have to imagine it. If you were to ask me straight questions I could probably give a straight answer, though.

After bathing we'd sun ourselves on the rug until we got too hot and had to go back into the water until we got too cold again. On the rug we'd lie side by side and talk, and get startled and panicky every time that we thought we heard somebody coming.

She once explained to me why she behaved as irrepressibly as she did. She said, 'I was born to be young. In fact I was born to be exactly the age that I am now, and that's why I want to make the most of it, because I know it can't last. One day I am going to have to make grown-up decisions, and be sensible. I'm going to have to find work and a flat to live in, I'm going to have to count the coins and pay the bills. One day I'll see wrinkles appearing around my eyes, and my breasts will start to sag, if they ever get to grow big in the first place, and sometime I'll have to find a promising man to marry, and the man will want me to iron his shirts, and then the part of me that tells me to be crazy will die so slowly that I mostly won't notice it happening, and then one day I'll look in the mirror and see my mother looking back at me, and then these times with you will seem like a beautiful dream that happened to someone else.'

As for me, I was too sensible already. I worked hard at school. I liked learning a lot more than I liked doing. I looked at the world through a sheet of glass.

One day she kissed me for a second time. She leaned over me, so that her blonde wavy hair fell about my face, and her skin was very hot from the sunshine. She touched my lips with hers very softly, and then pulled away, sitting up and clasping her knees in her arms. She said, 'There's so much to find out. The question is, is it all worth knowing?'

We lay side by side on the rug, Tasha lamenting the passage of time. We heard a bird singing nearby, and she said, 'It'll probably die of starvation in the winter.'

I said, 'Tasha, don't cry.'

We used to walk home in the evening, carrying the basket between us, and at night she slept in bed with me. Those were more innocent days, and no one thought anything of sharing a bed with someone of the same sex, if there weren't enough beds to go round. My parents thought that we looked very appealing curled up together. She was sweet and warm, her hair tickled my face, and when she was asleep she was so limp that I could move her into any position that was comfortable for me. I felt very safe with her, and I began to experience her fear of passing time, because when a friendship is so sweet and close, it always opens up the possibility that it will not last forever. Sometimes I felt sad when she fell asleep before I did.

Yes, those were more innocent days, perhaps, but we were lovers of sorts for about a year. We both knew that we weren't lesbians, but we did all the things that lesbians do. It was a question of pleasure and affection, and learning. I don't regret it and I don't look back with any shame. I don't feel turned on when I remember the details, but I do remember the fun and the passion.

She found a boyfriend, of course, and our affair ended very suddenly. We both thought it was natural and inevitable, and for a while we carried on just the same, but without the sex. I was looking forward to trying it with a man one day, myself. I found out later that she'd introduced her new boyfriend to our place by the river, and I assume that they made love there. Years later I met him by coincidence in Split, and he told me that she'd eventually dropped him for a cavalry officer who'd then become a politician. He was still very melancholy about losing her, which I could well understand. If I had been a man I would have been mad with love for her.

I told Chris that it had been Tasha who was wise enough to see what was eating at my father.

Ever since I was little, I always used to crawl into my parents' bed first thing in the morning, and soak up the family warmth, and if I was having nightmares I'd sleep the whole night with them.

After my parents stopped being a couple, my father

sometimes slept in the spare room. I used to get in with him if he was home, because my mother could have me for the rest of the time, and I didn't want my poor father to feel left out.

One morning when I was cuddled up next to him, kissing him on the cheek, I felt his whole body go rigid, and saw that he'd begun to sweat. I think that I'd been crying about something. He suddenly sighed and said, 'Roza, please don't come into this bed any more. You're no longer a little girl.'

'But, Papa,' I said, trying to protest, and he stopped me: 'Just go back to your room, and don't argue.'

I felt utterly miserable. At the door I turned to look at him, and my eyes filled with tears, but he'd turned over and was facing the wall.

After that I felt wounded and rejected every time that I saw him, and I sat for hours biting my knuckles and wondering what it was that I'd done wrong. My mind went blank and I couldn't come up with any answers, but I felt that everything between us had been spoiled.

I poured my heart out to Natasha, and she immediately jumped to the correct conclusion: 'Well, you aren't a little girl any more, and you're very pretty. Your father may be your father, but he's still a man. If you put a pretty girl in bed with a man, it's like putting food in front of a dog. I mean, it's a temptation.'

'But he's my father!'

'Yes, but listen. You love him and he loves you, and you're very pretty, and you're in the same bed. What do you expect? He had to throw you out, and obviously he couldn't explain why. If I were you I'd go home and take him a present, and stop getting into bed with him.'

I bought him a calculator. They were a novelty back then, and hadn't been in the shops at all long. They were still quite expensive. He said, 'I'll always treasure this, even if I never find out how to use it.' In fact his favourite use for it was to prove that he could do the sums quicker by mental arithmetic than I could by pressing the buttons. It became something that we did in order to impress visitors.

He bought me a tape of Françoise Hardy, saying, 'I don't know what kind of rubbish you youngsters are listening to these days, but this might help improve your French.'

I said, 'But I'm doing English and Russian,' whereupon he replied, 'In that case your French could do with a lot of improving.'

Over the years I got to love that tape, even though I didn't understand the songs until the Bob Dylan Upstairs talked me through them as we played it one day. Anyway, I liked the sweet sorrowful voice, whether I understood it or not. In the end the tape got chewed up in my cassette player, and I buried its remains in the park because it was too precious to throw away.

When Tasha found the boyfriend, it became difficult for us to spend so much time together. She sent me numerous confidential progress reports, and we spent long hours on the telephone, but I knew that she'd been stolen away, and that her beauty and humour belonged to someone else. The Bob Dylan Upstairs once played me a French song where the singer says that solitude is his most faithful companion, and will be his last, and I recognised the feeling.

I worked hard at my exams, and I went out looking for dogs to throw sticks for, but after Tasha I was very empty in the heart.

13
Poor Daddy

I just didn't want to be a virgin any more.

When I next visited, the door was answered by the Bob Dylan Upstairs, who by now had stopped wearing his black armband, but was still very morose. I'd just heard on my car radio that President Bhutto had been hanged in Pakistan, but I was right to assume that it was something else that was bothering the BDU.

Roza told me that the BDU had invited a beautiful and original and athletic girl to dinner, and had made her something special in his wok. I thought it would have been hard to have a romantic dinner in a house where the wiring was hanging off the walls, there were stair treads missing, the carpets were congealed with grease, and there wasn't a proper roof, but those kinds of young people had different standards, I suppose. It turned out that after dinner the girl had said, 'I hope you're not expecting any gymnastics, because Moira's my lover.'

The Bob Dylan had assumed that this Moira was just a flatmate. He had been very besotted with his dinner guest, and had definitely been hoping for some gymnastics. I know the feeling, I thought.

Roza, on the other hand, chose this day to tell me about some gymnastics of her own.

She said that she'd entered into a period when she was very depressed. It happens to lots of teenagers, I told her. My own daughter gets like that sometimes. No, said Roza, this was particularly horrible, because life lost all its meaning.

She stopped doing anything very much, became surly and hostile, and spent all day in bed, so that at night she had insomnia. The world was two-dimensional, like a cinema screen, and she became detached from it.

She told me that she kept thinking 'What for? Why bother?' and started to write poetry all about suicide and nothingness. She visualised what it would be like having her parents and Tasha standing by her graveside in the rain. She took to wearing nothing but black, and was very peeved when her father said that it suited her. She painted her room dark purple, and painted a mushroom cloud on the wall, around the bullet holes left over from the war.

She ostentatiously read Baudelaire in front of her parents' guests when they were expecting her to be sociable, and read books about psychology. I'd heard the name but I didn't know anything about this Baudelaire, so I went and found out afterwards. I am afraid I like best the poems about cats, and there's a very striking one about a corpse. She started reading Freud, and accused her father of being an anal retentive. He just said, 'Come into the toilet when I've had a shit, and I'll show you something to the contrary.' I had to look up 'anal retentive' as well. It's not a phrase or concept for which I have subsequently found much use, I have to say.

I said to Roza, 'What you've described is just a typical

teenager of a certain type.' She looked at me with some irritation, because no doubt she'd been expecting me to take her afflictions seriously. 'It was a crap time,' she insisted. 'I never felt so crap in my life, not even when I got raped.'

'Oh God,' I thought, but I knew her well enough by now. I knew she'd tell me sooner or later, so I didn't press her, even though she must have wanted me to. I definitely didn't want to ask her about being raped. The thought of it made me feel sick inside.

She went and fetched some more cigarettes, and I looked at the way that the paper was peeling off the walls. It was probably a pattern from Edwardian times, I thought. It must have been quite smart, once. The cracks on the ceiling made a map of the Isle of Wight. When she returned, clutching her pack of Black Russians, I said, 'So how did you get out of the depression?'

She lit up and leaned forward, her elbows on her knees. She looked at me coquettishly, tilted her head, blew out some smoke, smiled and said proudly, 'The night before I went to university, I went into my father's room, and we had sex.'

'Oh Christ,' I thought.

She said, 'It was my idea. I got into his bed and cuddled up to him just like the old days. But this time I knew what I was wanting. He couldn't help himself. He never got over it, I don't think. It was very mean of me. Poor Daddy.'

14
University

You've got to be careful of strangers.

The next time I saw Roza, she seemed very pleased with herself about something, but I didn't know what it was. As for me, I'd sold a walnut dresser for fifty pounds.

After what she'd told me I was beginning to wonder whether I wasn't risking too much. Someone who seduces her own father and thinks it's amusing is a dangerous person. Even so, I couldn't get over the fascination, and if anything it was getting worse. I was lying there sweating every night, and sleep was almost impossible until I was utterly exhausted. I'd be playing in my mind, over and over again, a sort of film in which I was both the actor and the director, and I was making love to Roza, and she was doing things to me that my wife had irrevocably given up fifteen years ago. The constant state of arousal was unbearable. It was a kind of dizziness.

I'd done something I wasn't proud of, but I was very glad it had happened. I'd been to practices in Watford and all sorts of places like that, and then I'd dropped in to see a friend of mine in Muswell Hill. It was late, and I was on my way home to the slumbering Great White

Loaf. I made a detour, and late at night I'd gone and stood outside Roza's house, on the other side of the street. It was May, so it wasn't too cold, and I just skulked in a doorway, in the shadows, as if I was a private eye. What I expected to come of it, I don't know, but I felt a certain satisfaction in seeing her shadow moving about behind the curtains. They were pink, and they can't have had any lining.

She started to undress. I saw all her characteristic movements, in silhouette. Then she pulled her sweater over her head, and I saw her reach behind to unhook her brassiere. She slipped it off and then she came to the window. I could see the silhouette of that curving, well-built body, approaching the curtains. To my amazement, and even to my horror, she opened the curtain and looked out over the street. For a moment I was frightened that she'd seen me, or knew I was there, but she just looked up and down the street. I saw her upper belly and her breasts very clearly in the light of the street lamp, heavy and rounded, and they became another reason not to sleep. I discovered before long that she went through this little ritual every night at about the same time. I was surprised that I was the only one who'd found out. I would have expected a whole crowd of us to be hiding in the shadows. I didn't want to become a pathetic peeping Tom. I felt I was being disrespectful to Roza, and I managed to stop myself from going too often. In fact I made a point of getting home early sometimes, so that it wouldn't look so bad when I was out late.

Roza told me that the Bob Dylan Upstairs had had another misfortune. He'd started seeing a pretty little blonde called Sarah, but this Sarah was living with a Dutch alcoholic called Hans. Sarah and Hans supposedly had an open relationship, but Hans had gone to pieces as soon as he'd heard about the Bob Dylan, and was drinking so much that Sarah was talking about ending their little fling, so the Bob Dylan was quite despondent again.

Roza was very chipper, however. 'Where did I get to?' she asked, and I said, 'You were just going to university.'

'After I slept with my father?'

'Yes,' I said, 'after that.'

'I had a shit time in Zagreb,' she said. 'The university was quite nice. It was a huge brown rectangle with wide corridors, and it was full of staircases. I wish I'd gone to Belgrade though.

'My father didn't come to the station. He couldn't even look at me when I went in to say goodbye to him. He was completely wordless, and he couldn't raise his arms to give me a hug. I hugged him, though. Tasha and my mother saw me off from the platform, and Tasha gave me some little handkerchiefs that she'd embroidered herself. My mother gave me a little parcel with the most amazing variety of foods in it, including a jar of preserved plums, in case I got constipated.

'On the train I started to cry, and an old man gave me his handkerchief. He said, "Keep it, my wife has been trying to throw it away for years, and I'm tired of fishing it out of the bin." I've still got it for crying into.

'I remember looking out over the fields of maize and sunflowers, and seeing herds of horses galloping, and sometimes a terrible smell of pigshit came into the train, and you'd look out, and you'd see all sorts of different-coloured pigs.

'You know what I wanted from university? I wanted parties, and rock music, and lots of intellectual things. I thought maybe I could be a professor myself one day. And I wanted a proper boyfriend, now that I wasn't a virgin.

'Well, I didn't get much of parties and rock music, and I didn't get much intellectual stuff, but I got the boyfriend straight away.

'When I got to the station I didn't know what to do, and it was dark, and I had all that luggage and food. I just wanted to go home again. I felt as if I'd landed on the moon. All the writing on the public spaces was in Roman script instead of Cyrillic.

'But I saw someone using a public telephone, and he looked quite nice, and I thought, "I bet he's a student." He was a bit thin, but he had lots of dark hair, and he wore a leather jacket. I went and stood nearby, but not so as he'd think I was eavesdropping, and when he'd finished on the phone I said, "Excuse me, but do you know where this is?"

'He took the paper and looked at it, and said, "Hang on a minute, I'm not used to joined-up Cyrillic. Haven't I seen you somewhere before?"

'I said, "Isn't that supposed to be a very corny line?"

'"Oh," he said, "I shall withdraw it then. I thought it was worth a try. Anyway, I am Alex, second-year engineering, and your hall of residence is right next to mine. It's just a question of catching the right bus. Shall I take one of your bags?"

'I said, "Oh, no, please don't worry," and he said, "I

know I'm a Croat, but you don't have to suspect me of anything."

'"I don't care what you are," I said, because in those days I really didn't. "You've got to be careful of strangers, that's all."

'He got out his identity card and his student card, and showed them to me. I gave him a bag, and he picked it up and said, "Jesus, what have you got in here, a corpse?"

'"I bought books in advance. I'm doing maths."

'"That's a bonus. You can help me out. I'm not much good at it, but I can't do engineering without it. Come on, it's not far to the bus."

'He came all the way to my room and carried my bags up the flights of stairs, then he stood at the doorway and said goodbye, and I saw that he had a very beautiful smile.

'I unpacked all my things and hid the cases under the bed and on top of the cupboard, and I sat at the little table and played with my pen, as if I was practising being a scholar. I went into the kitchen and introduced myself to all the other girls I was sharing with. I thought they were all very friendly and nice, but in the morning I found a bit of paper that had been slipped under my door, and it said, "*Dirty Serb go home.*"'

15
Alex

He took me to a place that was complete shit.

I heard that the Russians have a proverb about us Yugoslavs. It goes, 'Where there are two Yugoslavs there are three factions, and that's just the communists.' They say we're all just bandits and we've only got loyalty to our relatives, and we make pacts with our enemies just to take advantage of our neighbours. Anyway, someone once wrote '*Long Live Ustase*' on my door, but I didn't have too much trouble after that. I never had any time for all that tribal crap until I realised that all the other tribes hated me, no matter what. My best friend was Slovene, Tito was a Croat, my father's car was German, my watch was Russian, my camera was East German, and it was the British who freed us in the war. That's how I saw it back then. I thought, 'Who cares about all that stuff in the past?' Then the past jumps up and bites you in the leg, the moment you step back towards it. Nowadays I hate lots of people, but I don't do it seriously. I mean, I hate the Croats now, but I'd be happy to meet one any time, and I hate the Bosnians for breaking up my country, but I had a lovely friend who was Bosnian.

She was called Fatima. It was on the guided tour that

they make you go on to acquaint you with the university. There were lots of us. All the boys had brand-new military haircuts from their mothers, and the girls all had new plastic shoes that squeaked. I don't think any of us managed to remember all the historical facts they were telling us, and we still got lost for weeks afterwards.

Fatima had gold bangles on one wrist, and a shirt with no buttons, an embroidered waistcoat, open sandals, and those huge baggy trousers that you tie round your waist with a sash. She had her hair tied up in a scarf, and she had big gold earrings. She was the only one there who had any colour to her, and I thought she was very exotic. To be honest, I was surprised to see her at university because the Muslims usually kept their girls at home. I think it was much harder for Fatima at Zagreb than it ever was for me. She got pictures of pigs passed under her door at night. For a long time it was almost impossible for me to say anything to her without her thinking that I was insulting her in some elaborate and indefinable way. I suppose I persisted because I was naturally drawn to her. She once told me that what mattered wasn't religion, it was class. She was setting up a business with her husband, and so she'd come to get qualified in economics and administration.

I was a true communist back then, and I said I didn't believe in class. Fatima said, 'You want us all to be serfs and factory workers. I want us all to be aristocrats.'

Fatima and I spent a lot of time in the botanical gardens. We did all the tourist sites, and sat in all the right cafés. She smoked one cigarette a day, in a state of near ecstasy. She said she got the idea from reading an article about an American film star.

We liked the upper city. It had eighteenth-century mansions and palaces, and the Lotsrcak bell rang every day at noon. We sat on the cathedral steps, and talked about Matija Gubec, the one who got killed there when they crowned him with a white-hot circle of iron. Fatima said that the man who did it had a tomb in Stubica that is always damp because it drips with his sweat as he burns in hell. I said I didn't believe in hell, and Fatima tutted with her tongue and waved her hand dismissively. I think that she would have become an even better friend than Tasha, but what happened was very similar. Tasha got taken away from me by a boy, and that's how I got taken away from Fatima.

I was in the library when someone behind me said, 'Haven't I seen you somewhere before?'

He was still wearing his black leather jacket, and his hair still wasn't washed. He said, 'I knew I'd bump into you again. Listen, would you help me with a problem?'

I thought, 'Oh God, he wants to tell me something personal,' but he put a book down in front of me and said, 'It's problem three. It's to do with mechanical stresses when you've got three different forces acting in different directions. I don't really understand the formula for working it all out, and I thought that you might be able to help. My brain is turning into a walnut.'

I said, 'You've got to use differentiation with this problem. Do you know how to do that?'

'Not really. But if you show me I'll buy you a drink.'

He was smiling ironically, and I suddenly realised what he was up to. I said, 'You know perfectly well how to do this, don't you?'

'I had to have some excuse to approach you. And you do owe me a favour. For carrying your cases.'

He took me to a place that was complete shit. It was a sort of old cellar, and on the floor there was a thick slime of beer and ash. The toilets were all overflowing, and there were so many people that you had to hold your drink over your head. We had to shout to hear each other, and the smoke was so thick that it choked you, even if you were a smoker of Drina cigarettes, which I was at the time. It was the kind of cigarette that performs a tonsillectomy all on its own.

There was a band playing, and they were so loud and so bad! Later on, when I heard punk in England, it sounded very familiar. Someone threw their beer over the singer, and the singer hit him with the microphone stand. Then all hell broke loose, and soon there was a complete brawl. I wanted to get out, but Alex wanted to watch the fight, so I went outside and waited for him. The cold fresh air was like a kiss from an angel. I felt angry and pissed off, but on the other hand it had been quite an adventure.

When Alex eventually came out, his eyes were shining, and he said, 'Wasn't that brilliant?'

I said, 'No, Alex, it was pure crap. If you ever take me to anything like that again, you can consider me an ex-friend.'

'It was a bit alternative,' he conceded.

That night I went to the window of my room and saw Alex down below, hanging about underneath a street lamp, smoking a cigarette. I was touched, because it was a bit like Romeo and Juliet, and I waved to him. He waved back, and I realised afterwards that by then I'd already taken my top off. I just hoped that I'd been in shadow and that he hadn't seen anything. He certainly never mentioned it. I got a little kick out of it, though.

Alex brought me flowers to make up for the awful concert, but I didn't sleep with him for two months. Fatima often came with us, which I suppose might have annoyed Alex a lot, but he never showed it. We went to museums, and once we went to the opera, but it was obvious that Alex hated it. Anyway, I came to trust him, and I thought we were good friends.

One evening we were out in the snow, in the lamplight. I was wearing his hat, and he was doing a stupid dance as he pretended to be avoiding my snowballs. My hands got so cold that they started to ache, and I said I thought they were going to drop off, so we went indoors to my room, and just when he was rubbing my hands to warm them up, there was a standard government-issue power cut.

It went completely dark, and we started stumbling around looking for candles. Every time I lit a match to look for them, he'd creep up and blow it out, and we were laughing like idiots. In the end I lit a candle, which gave off a soft yellow glow. Normally the room seemed too small, but now it seemed intimate and very comforting. The peeling paint cast small flickering shadows behind the torn bits, and it seemed very bohemian and romantic.

I said, 'This is nice,' and he said, 'Now we can't do any work. Let's say thank you to the electricity man.'

'Thank you, electricity man,' I said. There was an awkward silence because we both knew what was likely to happen. Just for something to do, I went and put on the Françoise Hardy tape, but of course the player didn't work, so I switched it over to run on batteries. When I turned round, he was right behind me, and he caught me and kissed me very softly on the forehead. I let myself sink into his arms, and laid my head on his chest. I had the feeling that he was taking in the smell of my hair. After a while I lifted my face, and he kissed me properly. He had his eyes closed, but when he opened them they were glowing.

He went to the bed, sat on it, and held his arms out. He was smiling. I thought I ought to resist, but it didn't seem right somehow. I went to him, and he said, 'I adore you, Roza. I've been burning up inside ever since I saw you at the station.'

It was love at first sight, so I was flattered and pleased. He started to undo my buttons. It was leisurely. He kissed every new bit as he exposed it. He kept saying, 'You're so beautiful.' Eventually he was kissing me all over, and I felt I was in a delirium. He'd got all my clothes off without me even realising it properly, and I was beyond help.

He stood up and took off his clothes very quickly and efficiently, and then he was beside me, with his hands all over my body. He turned me over and stroked my back and the backs of my legs, and then he turned me onto my back. I said, 'I don't want to get pregnant.' My voice seemed very small and distant to me.

He got up and went and fumbled in his trouser pocket, and came back with a little packet. He said, 'I won't tell the new Pope if you don't.'

I felt a terrible disappointment. 'You were expecting

me to sleep with you? You were counting on it, so you got one of those?'

'We were both expecting it,' he said, 'or am I mistaken?'

'It's still not very nice. It makes me feel cheap.'

He came back to the narrow little bed, and said, 'Well, we can wait. Next time. Some other time. I don't want to spoil it.'

He took my right hand and started to stroke himself with it. I'd never have expected such a thing, but I didn't think of stopping him. I didn't want to. It was as if he was showing me how to please him. My hand took in all the beautiful textures and temperatures. He told me that my hand was cool and delicious. In the end I said, 'Let's not wait.'

When he was on top of me I was watching his face. He had his eyes closed, and I would have said that he'd turned into someone else, or was possessed. I liked the power I had. When he finished he slumped on me for a moment, and then he went back up on his arms and said, 'Christ, I felt like a god.'

The power came back on and spoiled the moment, but he turned off the lights to restore candlepower, and for a while we slept in each other's arms. We made love two more times that night, but it was quite a while before I learned to come with him, maybe three months. Alex was very good.

I always think that it was with Alex that I really lost my virginity. Everything else, Tasha and my father, was just practice.

16

Can You Fall in Love if You've Been Castrated?

CHRIS: I felt diminished when Roza told me about her romantic experiences. I think perhaps she didn't realise how much I wanted her. If she did, then she didn't have any regard for my feelings. It was my fault, I suppose. I could have stopped her, but I was fascinated. I was a voyeur with pangs of jealousy. It was foolish, because no one is without a past, but maybe it's better to pretend that every beginning is the first one. I would think about Roza being in love with Alex and having wonderful sex with him, and it made me think that I was an old nobody by comparison.

ROZA: I was watching his reaction when I was telling him the Alex story. He was uncomfortable, but I quite enjoyed that. It was fun tormenting him a little. I was stirring him up, and it was having a similar effect on me. When I said goodnight to him he was very subdued, and I kissed him on the cheek and gave him a medium-length hug, to keep him encouraged. He went home to his wife, and I wondered once again what it was like being married to him.

CHRIS: Next time I went I took her some flowers,

and I think she was really quite touched. It was only a bunch of yellow chrysanthemums, but her eyes lit up and her lip trembled a little. She was confused by it, and didn't know what to do. She glanced around that filthy hallway, as if she were looking for a vase, and then she clutched them to her chest, and said, 'You're so nice. You make me feel very good.'

I shrugged, as if to say, 'It was the least I could do.'

ROZA: I suppose it was cruel but when we were sitting downstairs in the basement I told him that Alex used to bring me yellow chrysanthemums. It wasn't true, though. I don't think he ever gave me much. Looking back I think he was probably screwing lots of women, and I doubt if any of them got much. I may be talking like a prostitute, but I don't really see the point of screwing someone who never gives you presents. Maybe it's because it gives you the feeling that you're still being courted, even though you've already been fucked half to death, and there's not much more to look forward to.

CHRIS: Roza kept telling me about her old boyfriend Alex. I don't know if she was tormenting me on purpose, to make me jealous, or whether she was just treating me as a confidant, a kind of tolerant uncle.

She said that her friend Fatima used to keep warning her about Alex, but she put it down to Islamic puritanism, and just ignored it. As for me, I think it's all very well getting moralistic about other people's sexual behaviour, and it's the easiest thing in the world to use one's principles as an excuse for cowardice. Now that I'm old

I just wish I'd been more of a rake when I was young. I wish I'd just followed my balls into battle, instead of sitting about thinking of reasons not to take risks and make memorable mistakes. I didn't even make a tentative start until middle age. You can't make love to beautiful girls when you're dead. When I lie dying I ought to be mulling over my most dramatic and ecstatic memories, but I hardly have any. I've wasted my life being sensible when I should have been cavorting and gallivanting. I haven't had enough bliss, I've just had one damned day after another, nice and calm, and now I've got bugger all to remember.

What I mean is that I don't blame Alex for whatever he was doing. I just wish that Roza hadn't made me suffer so much jealousy when she talked about him, especially as I was still reeling from what she'd told me about sleeping with her father. My feelings were boiling inside, and they were all contradictory.

ROZA: Alex used to arrive every evening at about nine o'clock, with a bottle of wine. We'd drink it side by side in that little bed, and then we'd make love. The other girls had to get used to him using the bathroom and making spaghetti in the kitchen. We used to talk for hours, setting the world to rights, just like proper students. I thought he was an idealist, and I admired him for it. I suppose I was too.

I told Chris that making love with Alex was like being God, because I could control him completely. I knew how to give him every kind of pleasure, so much pleasure that it almost made him suffer. I could make him moan and writhe about, and I could make him go wild, and he could do it to me too. I thought there'd never been lovers like us. Lovers often think like that.

It made my brain work better, all that sex. I did immense calculations and wrote long and complicated essays, and the professor said, 'One day you'll be after my job.' Once I even tried to read Einstein's little book on relativity, and I understood it at the time, even though I forgot what it had said the moment I'd finished it. It's funny to think that I could have been teaching at a university, instead of ending up with a life like mine, in a shitty slum house with no roof and half the stair treads missing.

CHRIS: Roza once asked me about my parents, and then told me about hers. That was the pattern of our conversations, really. Any curiosity about me was brought about by something that interested Roza in herself, and I sat listening so that I could just carry on appraising her body, looking at her in her tight white jeans, and wondering what her breasts would feel like if you cupped them, and whether she had big dark nipples or small delicate pink ones. If there's anyone who knows how to distinguish sexual obsession from love, they're a lot wiser than I am. If you had no sexual impulses, let us say, or if you had no hormones, would it be possible to fall in love? Can you fall in love if you've been castrated?

17
Breaking Up

People like things in theory.

She was in the middle of telling me about her university lover when she excused herself and went upstairs. When she came back down she showed me a letter. It was very old and yellowed, and the ink was a little faded.

'This is the letter my father wrote,' she said.

'I can't read it,' I said, perplexed.

'The point is,' said Roza, 'it's got splash marks on it.'

'Splash marks?'

'When he wrote it he was crying. You don't expect old partisans to be crying.'

'What does it say?' I asked.

She took it off me and translated: '"Dearest Printzeza, your mother and I have decided to divorce. I know that this will not come as a surprise to anyone, as we have not been happy together for years, but now that you and Friedrich have left home, it would seem to be the right time to make the break and start again. We are both getting older, and it will be difficult for both of us, especially for me, as I know that this failure is largely my own fault. Your mother is also writing to you, and I know that she will be able to express things better than I can. I will be staying at the house, and she will be moving into town so as to be closer to her friends. Dearest sweet Printzeza, there are so many things for which I beg you to forgive me, things that should not have happened. You know what I am talking about. Be assured that your mother and I will always continue to be united in our love for you. Your loving father."

'I got one from my mother, and that had tears on it as well,' she said.

'What happened to your father?'

Roza smiled and said, 'He did what Serbs always do. He got very depressed, drank slivovica and tried to kill himself with cigarettes.'

'I don't know anything about Serbs,' I said. 'You're my first one.'

'We get depressed, drink slivovica, and try to kill ourselves with cigarettes,' said Roza. 'It's our national way of life.'

'What did you do?'

'I got depressed and tried to kill myself with cigarettes. I missed out the slivovica. I went and talked a lot with Fatima, and she gave me lemon tea and a lot of talk about fate. She was a proper Muslim. Everything was God's will. I thought, 'No, it's not,' but Fatima was good with me. Alex was OK as well. He was nice to me. I didn't know he'd been seen kissing some other girl on Beogradska Avenija, because no one told me till later.

'He got a motorbike and we went out to the Zagrebacka Gora. It's all mountains and forests, and you go with a gun because there are still bears and wolves and big wild pigs. We used to go to Sestine and then into the remote places, so we could make love on a rug. If I ever got bored making love with him, I just imagined it was my father.'

When she said that, I winced. She just blew out some smoke, and smiled. 'You're funny,' she said. She paused. 'You know what, Chris? After my parents separated, Alex asked me to marry him.'

'What did you say?'

'I said "yes". I didn't know he was fucking around. I don't know why he asked me.'

'You can love someone and still want to sleep with other people,' I said. 'It's normal. It isn't romantic, but it's normal.'

'I was a romantic when I was young,' she said, and I thought, 'How romantic is it to seduce your own father?' but I didn't say anything.

'Anyway, when I said "yes" it put him in a panic. I think he'd been hoping I'd refuse.'

'Why did he ask then?'

'People like things in theory,' she said. 'Maybe I want to go to the Amazon, look at all those parrots and trees. If I got the chance, I'd say, "Oh how wonderful," and then I'd be working out how not to go there, because really I don't want to go to the Amazon and get too hot and be eaten by mosquitoes after all. Maybe I'd rather be in Archway in this little shithole.' She took a sip of tea, and lit another Black Russian. 'Anyway,' she said at last, 'it was then that everything went wrong. Fatima said it would. She said he'd end up marrying a nice Catholic virgin, and he'd be unfaithful all his life, and he'd die wishing he'd married me after all. I told her to shut her mouth, what did she know? And then we had the summer holidays.

'I went home and saw what was happening with my father. He was living like a pig. Dirty clothes everywhere. Dust and filthiness. All the cupboards with everything emptied out and not put back. Grey sheets on the bed, and bottles outside the door, and piles of newspapers. I tell you what, my father was defeated, and it made me feel very bad and very sorry. He was eating only sandwiches, and when I made him papazjanija, he ate it like a wolf. I said to him, what happened to the old partisan who knows how to live off rats? And he said, "I was alive back then." I was showing him how to pick up dust with a damp cloth, and how to boil up kitchen cloths, and how to use lemon and salt to clean brass. I showed him how to choose the good fruit in the market, and to look at the eyes of a fish to see if it's fresh, and how to tell the weight of things, and I said to him, "You lived with Mama all that time and you never saw what she was doing?" I said, "Listen, Daddy, you should invite friends for a meal one evening every week, and that'll force you to clear up a bit," and you know what? That's what he did. And I got a job in the little tourist office next to the Albania building, and I spent the summer being too hot and trying to understand people with all sorts of accents. And one night I came home and my daddy said, "Do you remember when you were about six, I made you stand out in the snow in your nightdress, because you scribbled on some documents?" And I said, "I thought I was going to die," and he said, "Printzeza, I've always meant to say I'm sorry," and I said, "I've got things I'm sorry about," and he gave me a hug and went and stood outside in the garden in the dark, and I looked through the window and saw him standing under the cherry tree with his cigarette end glowing. I told him I was getting married to Alex, and he just said, "Try and live somewhere nearby. For God's sake don't stay in Croatia," and I said, "Don't worry, Daddy, it's not far on the train."

'I went into the village and hired someone called Mrs Kidric to come and clean the house one day a week. I went home and told my daddy he'd have to pay her, and that was that. She was good, she made a big effect. She was like a weightlifter and she walked like a goose, she had moles and a beard, and she had the Partisan Star because she'd strangled a German soldier with her bare hands during the Siege of Belgrade. When she'd done the house she used to take a drink with my father at the kitchen table, and they talked about the war and sang old songs.

'Sometimes I went to the place by the river where Tasha and I used to swim and fool around with no clothes on. I felt some sweet nostalgia. One day I saw her old boyfriend, and he said he used to go there with her sometimes, and I thought, "Shit." It was his special place too, and I didn't like it. That's when I heard she'd gone off with the handsome cavalry officer. He said, "I'm just a trainee manager in a canning plant," and shrugged his shoulders. I thought he was nice. I said, "Tasha wouldn't ever hurt anyone on purpose, you know," and he just snorted.

'I went to see Mama quite a lot, but there wasn't much point. She'd decided to get old as quickly as she could, and she just wanted to dry out and disapprove of everything. That was her pleasure, to disapprove of things. She'd become very religious, and she gave me a Bible, and I got halfway through all the lists of atrocities in the Old Testament, and gave up. I thought, "I can take it when some politician says we've got to go out and kill people, but I'm not taking it from God. He ought to know better." What do you think, Chris?'

After such a long speech, I was surprised to be addressed. I said, 'God and I have an agreement to leave each other alone. I don't bother Him and He doesn't bother me. If we meet in the street we raise our hats and smile and give each other a wide berth. So what happened when you went back to university?'

Roza pulled a wry face, and said, 'I was phoning him all summer and hardly ever got through. He didn't like phoning anyway. Men don't like phones. When I got back I discovered he had a new girlfriend, and she looked just like me, and I couldn't believe it. I thought, "What? What is this man, that he gets another one just like me?"

'Anyway, I was happy at first when I got back to Zagreb, and I got a bottle of wine, and I thought, "We'll drink this in bed and make love till we can't do it any more." I got some flowers to take to my room, and I phoned him up and I waited for his footsteps outside in the corridor. He put his right foot down much harder than the left one, so he wore out the right shoe first. You knew it was him from the rhythm. When he arrived I threw my arms around him and kissed him all over his face, and I put my hand in his trousers and dragged him into the little bed, and I gave him a blow job and he fucked me twice before he told me about the other girl.'

At this point Roza fell silent. I said, 'I'm very sorry. It must have been completely awful.'

'Fucking bastard,' she said, 'fucking fucking bastard. You know what he said? He said I was too good for him, and I should get someone better. He said I was too much for him, like I was a hurricane or something. He even cried a bit. Bastard. You know what I did? I walked around the city every night and I didn't eat, and I got thin like a ghost, and I was biting my lips and making them bleed, just like my mother, and he sent me a little note that said, "*Roza, I am very sorry. Thanks for all the good times. Alex.*" You know what? I wanted to kill him. That was all I could think about. If I saw him at the university I wanted to stick my fingers in his eyes. In the end I called round at his place, and I went in and wrecked it.'

'Wrecked it?'

Roza smiled with satisfaction. 'I broke it all. Everything. Everything smashed.'

'Didn't he try to stop you?'

'I was a hurricane, just as he said. He just stood there and couldn't do anything, and then when I left I picked up his favourite record, and I went outside and I broke it into four pieces and I posted them back under the front door. It was the Rolling Stones. "Honky Tonk Woman".'

'I must remember not to annoy you,' I said.

'I went home and cried in my room, and then decided to leave. I had an idea I must go to England.'

'You didn't finish your degree?'

'My professor begged me. He said I was the best. I said, "I'm going anyway," and he said, "Your place is open. Come back soon." The day before I left he made me a chocolate gateau and left it outside my door, and there was a note saying, "*I bet you can't eat it in one go. My wife helped me make it.*" I took it to Marulicev Park, and I did eat it all in one go, except I gave some to the birds. I'll tell you one good thing that happened because of Alex.'

'Oh, what was that?'

'It made me write poems. I was a mathematician, but I wrote lots of poems and I never stopped, and one day I'll go home and I'll get them in a book. Then I'll be a poet, and every day I'll be thinking, "Thank you, Alex, you fucking bastard." Anyway, I went and drank lemon tea with Fatima for the last time, and I never saw her again. She gave me a gold bangle and a gold ring, and she said they were from her dowry, but it didn't matter, she wanted me to have them. I don't know what happened to her. She was married to a nice Muslim man and he probably turned out to be a fucking bastard like Alex.

'You know what? Leaving Zagreb was the stupidest thing I ever did in my life.'

18
Leaving

A broken heart travels with you.

The next time I saw Roza there was a lot to be depressed about. The Ayatollah Khomeini was saying that there wasn't going to be any democracy in Iran. Everyone was still on strike for preposterous wage rises, and the only good news was that Idi Amin had absconded. Everyone was singing some bloody song that you couldn't get out of your head called 'I Will Survive', but not many of us reckoned we would. Seeing Roza cheered me up, though. It was like visiting a butterfly house on a rainy day. The daffodils were coming up too, in between all the uncollected rubbish.

When I called round I could hear music coming from upstairs, and I recognised it as something my daughter was listening to at home. She made me listen to it, the way your children sometimes do, and there was a long and complicated guitar part, and I said, 'This man is a real musician.' She looked at me and said, 'Don't like it too much, Dad, or you'll put me off it.' I wish I could remember the name of the group, but the song was something about some jazz musicians called the Sultans of Swing. I still hear it on the radio sometimes, and it takes me back to those days, because for ages when I went round to see Roza you would hear the Bob Dylan Upstairs trying to work it out on an electric guitar.

I said to Roza, 'So what happened next? Did you come here straight away?'

She laughed a little bitterly and said, 'I went to bloody Bosnia.'

'Why?' I was trying to imagine a map of Yugoslavia, and to visualise where Bosnia was. It didn't work, so, as often before, I had to look it up when I got back to Sutton.

'I had big trouble at home. Both of them telling me I was crazy, and didn't I know I was messing up my life, and all those kinds of things. I just wanted to go away somewhere. I thought maybe if I went away I could leave myself behind. Flying away is for people who want to do a suicide without killing themselves.'

'It doesn't work?'

She shook her head. 'It doesn't bloody work. You have to take yourself along when you go. It didn't work in bloody Bosnia.'

'I thought you wanted to come to England.'

She pulled one of her wry expressions. 'I went to the embassy on Generala Zdanova. It works like this: you don't get a visa without a work permit, and you don't get a work permit without a visa, and you don't get either of them without a job, and you don't get a job without both of them. It's simple. Everyone said, "Look, Roza, what you do is go there as a tourist, and you spend time in a language school, and they give you permission to stay if you're studying English. Then you find some work because sooner or later somebody likes you and gives you a job." So I decided to do it like that, but I had to save up money first, and that's why I went to bloody Bosnia, because I got a job in a timber yard, working in the office.

'It was a shitty little place, like a village on the side of a hill with nothing but trees. Every morning at dawn the bloody muezzin woke me up and drove me crazy with all that wailing. I'd never had to live with Muslims before, and these ones weren't sophisticated like Fatima. I like it when you go to Sarajevo, they're modern people, but these ones, I didn't understand them, and they thought that I was shit. Some of them spat in the path of infidels. I thought, "Shit, I'm living with savages." All those years of living under Tito, and it hadn't made any difference.

'I had a little room above a bakery, and I was there all alone every evening after work, with no one to talk to and nothing to do except get angry with Alex. I couldn't go out because all the men thought I was available for a fuck, and I realised that the men called me "the cat" because of how I kept fighting them off, and the women called me "the bitch" because they thought I was trying to screw their husbands. I used to get men offering me money because they thought that if I was an infidel woman I must be a whore.

'Then one day something happened. It was on a public holiday, and I was just walking in the street when somebody shouted at me from the other side, and this skinny guy just ran over and started trying to kiss me. Anyway, I hit him. He said, "Your anger makes you more beautiful." I said, "Get lost," and he said, "When I saw you from across the street, I knew I had to make love with you. It was fate."

'"Oh bullshit," I said, and he said, "No no no, it's true. It's God's will. Can we go and talk somewhere? It's very necessary."

'I looked at him and thought that actually he looked quite nice. He had warm eyes. He said, "Where do you live?" and I made the mistake of pointing to my little room above the bakery. He just grabbed my arm, and he dragged me in there, right past the owners of the shop, and they did nothing at all even though I was in distress and it was bloody obvious. He said, "She's my little sister," and they just gawped like a couple of fish.

'Upstairs he pushed me into a corner with one hand, and he was trying to undress himself with the other, and he was talking all this rubbish that he must have got out of a poetry book, about how it was destiny, and I was one line in space and he was another, and now we were meeting because the lines were always bound to meet. I was just trying to get his hand off me, and I was thinking that I ought to scream for help, but somehow I was too embarrassed.

'Then he had to let go of me so that he could get his trousers off, and I took the chance, and I grabbed a lamp from the bedside table, and I was waving it at him and telling him to get out.

'He just looked at me and put his hand in his pocket and he brought out this big dirty roll of money. He offered it to me and said, "Look. For you." I tried to hit him with the lamp, but he got out of the way. He put his clothes back on and he just said, "Mad bitch, me and my brothers are going to come back and teach you something. You're not going to be waiting long, so don't worry, mad bitch, don't worry."

'In that kind of place those Albanians all have twelve brothers, and they all carry hunting rifles in public. They get into blood feuds and they do honour killings, and they live up to their threats, so I didn't sleep all night, and in the morning I packed up my things and I took the first bus to Sarajevo and then the first bus to Belgrade. Before I left I confronted the owners of the bakery. I said, "Why didn't you help me?" and the man said, "We stay out of things," and it was then that I realised that even for them I was just a piece of Christian shit even though I'd been paying rent and I wasn't actually even a Christian. I said, "You disgust me," and then I left. Ever since then I started hating those people, because it gives you no choice if they just think you're shit. I did two months in that shitty place, and if I never go back, it's a good reason to die a little bit happy.

'When I got home I went to see Miss Radic, and Tasha, and I went into town to see my mother a few times. I was waiting for my passport and exit permit, and I got my father to sign the papers because he thought I was only going to Italy. Alex and me, we used to have this fantasy about going to Dubrovnik or Trieste and getting work on a rich man's boat, and getting around like that. Lots of young people were doing things like that. I thought, "I'm going to do it anyway." As the Albanian said, I was just a mad bitch.

'One morning I got up after my father went to work and I tried to write him a long letter about what I was doing, but somehow I couldn't express myself. It was all covered with crossing-out, and the words and feelings got all jumbled and I kept wanting to cry, so I gave up. I went upstairs and I put my fingers in the bullet holes just as I did when I was little, and I looked at the bed where Tasha and I used to giggle all night, and I looked at my teddy bears, and out in the orchard I could see the old carthorse eating fodder, and I told myself, "It's OK, you'll be back in a year."

'I went into Belgrade to see my father, and I found out that it's difficult to get into an office when it's to do with state security. I could hardly get past the policeman at the door, and then the receptionist didn't want to phone up to my father's office. When I finally got there I was shocked by how small and cramped it was. I always thought my daddy was more important. There were piles of paper everywhere, and it hadn't been painted in years, and the filing cabinet had a drawer that wouldn't close. On the wall there was the usual picture of Tito, but it was all faded and the corners were turning up and a bit torn. There was a big black-and-white photograph of a beautiful young woman in partisan dress, and across the bottom, in big confident handwriting, it said, "*With all my love forever, Slavica.*"

'My daddy pointed at my suitcase and said, "I didn't know you were going today." I said, "Neither did I." He said, "I wish you would stay. You do know you'll get practically nothing for dinars, don't you? It's Italy, is it?"

'I couldn't bear to lie, so I said, "Maybe I'll try to get to England." He said, "Ah, I've always wanted to go to England. Winston Churchill. Big Ben. White cliffs. Spitfires and Hurricanes. Why don't you wait till my leave comes up? Maybe we could all go. We could take Tasha. You can't have enough money to get to England anyway. I've hardly got enough myself, and I've been working for years."

‘I said, “Papa, I’ve just got to go,” and he said, “You can go as far as you like, but a broken heart travels with you.”

‘“It’s only a holiday,” I said. Then I asked, “Who is Slavica?” and I gestured to the photograph.

‘“She got killed,” he said. “I expect we would have got married.” I looked at the picture of the lovely smiling girl and said, “Maybe you would have been happy,” and he said, “I wouldn’t have had you and Friedrich though.” I thought, “Shit, I owe my existence to the death of a pretty partisan sometime in the war.” It made me think that there must be millions of people like me, whose parents ended up with a miserable second choice. My daddy said, “She was rather like Tasha. She had the same kind of personality. I always have funny feelings when I see Tasha.”

‘“What happened to her?”

‘“The Ustase got her. You know what those people were like. Anyway, they wrecked her like you’d wreck a doll with a hammer, and they just hung the body over a fence. There wasn’t anything they hadn’t done.”

‘“Did you ever love Mama?”

‘“There are different kinds of love.”

‘It was a nice photograph of Slavica. She had a thin neck and eyebrows like little arches. Sad eyes. Her hair was in a ponytail. I could just imagine her voice.

‘My daddy took me to the bank and got some dinars out for me, and then he came with me to the bus station and bought me my ticket. He said, “You might miss the big event.”

‘I said, “What big event?” and he replied, “The Old Man’s dying.”

'"Oh," I said. I had always thought of Tito as immortal.

'"Yes," said my daddy, "and then everything will go to hell. Everything we fought for. I get lots of information coming through my office. The vultures are gathering. All the nationalists and the religious crazymen. They can see their chances coming. I don't give this country ten years when the Old Man goes. With any luck I'll be dead, because I don't want to live to see everything being shat on by shitheads. And you know what? The Old Man's been devolving power away from the centre. You'd think he'd know better than that."

'I said, "Don't be silly, Papa, everything'll be fine," and then I had to kiss him and say goodbye. I said, "Listen, Papa, I am really sorry," and he said, "Me too," and we both knew what we were talking about. I wasn't sorry for myself, just for what I'd done to him.'

19

Satisfaction

There aren't enough rhymes for 'love'.

The next time I saw Roza I was feeling uneasy because the Yorkshire Ripper had just killed another woman in Halifax. It wasn't a prostitute this time, though. Every time I heard about another victim, I thought about what could have happened to Roza if she'd stayed at the hostess club. I sometimes meant to ask her about it, but it seemed inconsiderate to mention that someone was going round cutting up prostitutes. She didn't bring it up, so maybe she wasn't even aware of it. She didn't follow the news much. She was interested in politics in a rather abstract way, but until I told her, she hadn't even known that the government had lost a vote of confidence and Callaghan was about to call a general election. She lived in her own little world, and it didn't include Mr Callaghan and the Yorkshire Ripper.

I brought her some chocolates, and she ate all of them, one by one, as she told me the next bit of her story. She let me have the ones with hazelnuts in, though. She had slightly gappy teeth, so she avoided nuts, or so she said.

The storytelling had become quite formal by now. I was just turning up for the next instalment. I simply had to say, 'You were going to tell me how you got to England,' and she was off into the next episode. I just sat there looking at her and thinking how much I wanted her. I'd found a five-pound note on the pavement in Seven Sisters Road, and I'd saved another twenty-five pounds, for my Premium Bond fund, and I was feeling optimistic. She said that she liked it when I was cheerful.

'If I'd had any sense,' she began, 'I would have just gone to Dubrovnik. It would have been a lot quicker and easier. But I'd decided to go from Trieste, and now I think the reason is that we had to go through Zagreb. It was because Alex was in Zagreb.

'You know, it was April, and the whole country was covered in flowers. It was beautiful to see, and the road was mostly following the Sava River, and that was very beautiful too.

'It was fun on the bus in Yugoslavia. It was like a picnic, and everybody brought too much food, and it got shared around. Some people had wine, and they were talking too loud and telling jokes. You didn't go on a bus for peace and quiet. Some people played chess. The driver had a tape of frula music, and one of a brass band, but he had another one too, and he played it over and over again all the way to Zagreb. It was "Satisfaction". Do you know that one?'

'I'm not sure,' I said. 'I expect my daughter knows it. I'll ask her when I get home.'

'It's the Stones,' said Roza. I could see she was incredulous that I didn't know it. I said, 'You mean the Rolling Stones?' and she said, 'Yes, the Rolling ones,' and rolled her eyes just as my daughter used to. 'How does it go?' I asked, and Roza looked at me as if I was mad and said, 'I can't do singing. You really want me to sing like Mick Jagger for you?'

'Oh well, I know about Mick Jagger,' I said.

'Oh good. Well, the thing is, the song goes, "I can't get no satisfaction."'

'That's awful grammar,' I said. 'That really means I have no alternative but to be satisfied at all times.'

'You complain to Mick Jagger, OK? Anyway, everyone was singing along, and some of the men were doing Mick Jagger impersonations, you know, leaping about in the aisle and pretending their Fanta bottle was a microphone, and so the driver kept rewinding it, and the men were puffing out their lips. Then we got stopped by the traffic police, and they told the driver off for allowing people to dance about in the bus. After that we all sat nice and quiet for half an hour, and then it all started again. You know what? Not many people were satisfied in Yugoslavia back then. For us it was a good song.

'Anyway, when we got near Zagreb and I saw the nice villas in the suburbs, I began to feel sick. At the bus station on Drziceva Avenue, I thought, "OK I'll get the bus to Trieste in a couple of hours, so I can go for a walk around." I thought, "Maybe I'll go and see Fatima," but then I realised no, it was Alex I wanted to go and see. I walked past one of the hotels and it had those prostitutes in the lobbies who only did it with tourists for dollars and Deutschmarks. I was walking by the cathedral when I thought, "I'm not going to go and see Alex." I'd been having this idea that maybe I'd go to his place and wreck it all over again, but now I thought, "I'm just too tired of all this stuff," and then I said to myself, "Come on, Roza, you're a partisan's daughter, you don't take any shit." Even so, I sat on the cathedral steps for a while, and then I went and had a coffee in a place I never went to when I was a student. Then I went and sat on the steps of St Mark's and watched the pigeons and smoked lots of cigarettes. I had all these tears that wouldn't come up, and my stomach was turning round and round. In the end I just went back to the bus station, and when we left for Trieste I was thinking, "Well, OK, Alex, fuck you forever." It was sad to leave Zagreb again, though.

'On the bus to Trieste an old man sat next to me. He said, "I hope you don't mind, but someone pretty like you will make me feel happy for a while if I sit next to her." I could tell he was a nice old man. He had those Drina cigarettes we were all killing ourselves with in those days, and he gave me some. He wanted to talk about whether or not there'd be another drought, because he'd lost all his aubergines in the last one. Then he asked me if I was scared of dying.

'I just wanted to be left alone, and to think about Alex, and I was feeling very nervous about going away without any plans, but I couldn't escape him. He just wanted to talk and talk and talk. But he said some things I remembered. He said that life was a walk through the cosmos, and at the end of the walk you're so tired that you don't really mind dying, all you want is a sleep. You know, I feel like that a lot, and I'm not even thirty. He told me he'd been an intellectual before the war, but now nobody listened to him any more, and he was just an old peasant. He said he'd fought in the Spanish Civil War, and if I ever went to Spain, would I please spit on Franco's grave for him? Then he said that one reason he wanted to go to Rome was because he wanted to spit on Mussolini's grave. I said I thought he didn't have one. I thought they'd just thrown him away or something. He said that mankind would never give up its suffering, because it liked suffering more than anything else, and that's why he'd given up being a communist. He said that each one of us was just a tiny molecule of snot up the great nose of life, and that he could die happy because at least his fields had more horseshit on them than they had when he started.

'I was just looking out of the window, wondering how a land as beautiful as Croatia could have produced a man like Alex.

'Then the old man fell asleep, and it gave me the same fear that I always used to have when my grandmother fell asleep in a chair, you know, the fear that she was dead. I kept listening to see if the old man was breathing or not. But he kept waking up at crucial moments and saying things like "Over there where you can't see it is a very pretty castle with six towers" and "Over there there's a village where a German general was assassinated, so they killed every male in the place, and now it's populated by old crones dressed in black, who don't let any men near the place. They look like ravens. Also the Germans removed the eyes of all the corpses and delivered them back in a basket. And you know what? They don't tell you this, but we Yugoslavs spent more time fighting each other than fighting the Axis. In the end I just went home. You know what? I had a wife and a daughter and a little son, and I just hid in a field when they were being killed. I could hear the screaming. All I had for a weapon was a spade."

'I said, "Why are you telling me this?" and he said, "Because you don't know me." He started to cry very quietly, so I just held his hand until we got to Ljubljana. It was dry like paper, and a bit twitchy. After Ljubljana he recited bits of his poems that he'd written before the war, and he told me a few jokes about Albanians, and he said there weren't enough rhymes for "love" and "beauty". I don't know why I am telling you all this. It's not important, it's just memories.'

I was surprised when she interrupted herself, and for a moment I couldn't think what to say. 'Obviously he made a big impression. I don't mind, I just like to listen to you. Maybe one day I'll tell you everything that's happened to me. If you can put up with the boredom.'

'I think about him a lot,' said Roza. 'I expect he's dead by now.'

'I suppose you last saw him at Trieste?'

'Yes. We said goodbye at the Piazza Libertà, you know, where the coach station is. He kissed me on both cheeks, and he said, "Remember about Franco, if you ever get the chance." He said he was going to go to a place nearby where there was a concentration camp in which twenty thousand got incinerated. That was his kind of tourism. He wanted to travel around being reminded that humans are basically shit. He said, "You make me wish I was twenty-five," and I said, "You make me wish I was seventy."

'You know what? I felt bad crossing the border. I'd never been abroad before. I suddenly felt like a traitor. I thought I'd go to the harbour, and if my courage failed me, I'd just go home again.'

I said, 'I'm amazed your father let you go off like

that,' and she said, 'If your daughter was twenty, could you stop her going away if she wanted to?'

I shook my head. 'But you didn't have a proper plan. You had nothing arranged.'

'I think my father had no authority. I took it away from him because of what happened. I think maybe he was relieved.'

'It sounds crazy to me.'

She laughed and looked at me coyly. 'But, Chris, you know I'm a crazy girl.'

'So did you get a boat in the harbour?'

'Not straight away. It was raining cats and dogs, as you people are always saying, and it said in my guidebook that there was a convent which made a living by having women and married couples to stay. I walked there in the rain. It was very cheap. There was a Virgin Mary statue everywhere you looked. You could hardly move for Virgins. I got depressed because of all the crucifixes with little Jesus Christs hanging on them. I don't like it, all those little skinny men being tortured, hanging up on the wall. Anyway, the nuns were very nice, and they gave me some pasta without any meat in it, and I went to bed and couldn't sleep.

'Trieste is just like Ljubljana. It didn't feel like abroad. It smelled of coffee, though, the whole town smelling of roasted coffee. It was lovely. You know what? They put ropes along the streets so you can pull yourself along when the wind's too strong. They've got a wind called bora, and it blows you over.

'You know what I did in the morning? I bought proper tampons, and toilet paper that doesn't scratch. Then I went down to the harbour, and I saw lots of big ships in the port, but everything else was a car park. I thought, "Shit, I should have gone to Dubrovnik," but then I found the place where the yachts were, all pretty and elegant, with their little flags and their wires slapping, rising and falling on the water. I sat down on my case and it made me feel happy just looking at the boats, and the sunlight on the water, sparkling, and if you looked out to sea you couldn't tell where the sky stopped and hit the water.

'Anyway, I walked around all the boats and if I saw someone I asked them if they wanted anyone to crew on the boat. I had to ask in English because I didn't know Italian, and nobody knows Serbo-Croat. I learned a little English in school, but it was crap. I learned things like "Oh what delightful weather" and "Do pass the sugar" and "Excuse me, but where can I find the library?"

'Nobody had any work, and I was thinking, "Shit, I'd better go home," when a man on a boat said, "I don't need anyone, but I think that Francis does. This is where his crew got off." I said, "Francis?" and he said, "You go a couple of quays along. It's an old boat called *Sweet Olivia Bunbury*." I said, "Where's he going?" and the man said, "Back home to England." I thought, "Yes! Maybe just this once God exists for Roza."

'I found the boat, and it was a nice old one, all dark wood covered in varnish, and sparkly brass things. There was a man winding a rope up on the deck, and he looked at me, and I said, "Are you Francis?" except that my English was much more crap back then, and I probably said, "Are you being Francis?" or something like that.

'He said, "That's me. Who's asking?"

'I said something like "I am being told that you have work. I am wanting to go to England."

'He said, "Have you got a passport?" and I showed it to him, and he said, "Have you got a visa? Don't you need a visa for Great Britain?" And I said, "Not if you're a Yugoslav." Really, I didn't know, but I said it anyway.

'He said, "What's your experience?"

'I didn't know the word, so he said, "Have you worked on a boat before?" and I said, "No, but I am not stupid. I learn."

'He looked at me as if I was mad, and said, "Sorry. I need people with experience."

'You know, I was so disappointed I sat down on my case, and I started to cry. And then he started cursing, and he carried on working on the boat, and I carried on crying. In the end he said, "Look, are you any good at cooking?" and I looked up and said something like, "I am a delightful cook," and he started laughing. He said, "OK, you cook something delightful tonight, and if you're any good I'll think about taking you on."

'I said, "What have you got?" and he said, "Look in the fridge." So I came up the gangplank, and he looked at my shoes before he'd allow me on deck. It was flat shoes only. Anyway, I went down and looked in the fridge and it was crap in there. Old stuff, and tins of old shit half eaten. I said, "You don't eat?" and he said, "Not if it's me cooking." I said, "You give me money, I'll go and buy food." He said, "You want me to give you money?" and I said, "Look, I'm leaving my case here. I don't go and be buying food with a case, do I, sir?" So he gave me some lire and I went away and I bought two mullet, and lots of nice vegetables, and rice and garlic and new bread, and proper food like that, and in the evening I made the mullet with the liver still in for the extra flavour, not overcooked like English fish, and I made prawns with lemon and garlic, and potatoes cooked very slow in olive oil and oregano, and I made a proper salad with olives and red onions in, and I found some nice wine. He ate all that, and he said, "Jesus Christ, Roza, I don't care if you don't know how to sail." You know, that's how I first learned about Englishmen and proper food. That's how you get what you want. They never ate properly when Mama was cooking, because English mamas can't cook, so if you cook a proper meal they're amazed and impressed. Anyway, that night I didn't go back to the convent, I slept in that little narrow bit right up at the pointed end.'

'And that's how you became crew?'

Roza nodded smugly. 'I learned sailing pretty bloody quick. He got somebody else as well, it was an Australian man with long blond hair and big muscles. He was nice. He had a mouth full of big white teeth. It made me think good things about Australia. He stayed as far as Palma, and by then I knew how to do it, mostly. Francis didn't find anyone else in Spain, and anyway it was too late.'

'Too late?'

'He was fucking me. He didn't want someone else on the boat to get in the way of the fucking.'

I hated it when Roza talked like that. I found it offensive. It was coarse and vulgar, and I didn't think that it reflected her true nature. She did it just for effect, with a kind of artificial casualness, and she always looked directly into my eyes because she was testing my reaction. In any case, I felt vicious pangs of jealousy when she talked about sex with anyone else. It hurt me to think about it. I said, 'You make it sound like you had nothing to do with it,' and she said, 'OK, I was fucking him too. I was fucking Alex out of my system, OK? And it was making love, it wasn't just fucking.'

'So, who was Francis?'

'Why? You think maybe you know him? OK, he was maybe about thirty, and he was very nice, and he was tall, and he had plenty of money. I liked him enough. I could have fallen in love with him maybe. He made me feel affectionate.'

'Did he fall in love with you?'

'Sure.' She pulled on her cigarette and tapped the ash into the ashtray on the greasy arm of her chair. Then she stubbed it out. 'Do you want to hear about being on the boat?'

I said, 'OK, tell me about the boat.'

'It had a little toilet and you had to pump it to make it fill up. And on the wall it said: "*Don't put anything in here that you haven't eaten first*", so it was OK for vomit anyway. Down there I always felt sick if the boat was moving. And there was a little sign by the wheel that said: "*The Captain's Word is Law*".'

I looked at my watch and realised I'd have to go if I wanted to miss the rush hour. In any case, I loathed the feelings that I was getting in my guts, so I said, 'Look, Roza, I'm afraid I've got to go. Can you tell me next time?'

She kissed me goodbye at the door. One kiss on each

cheek, and a kiss on the lips that almost seemed about to turn into a proper kiss. When I drove away in that shit-brown Allegro, and thought about that nearly-kiss, I felt a lot better.

20
Voyage

I never even killed a dolphin.

Mrs Thatcher came to power, and everyone was wondering what was going to happen. I wasn't sorry to see the end of Callaghan. I don't think anyone was. It was all very well having a nice man in charge, but he hadn't really been in charge. The most memorable thing he did was to sing 'My Wife Won't Let Me' at a conference. Roza didn't care one way or the other. Her only political concern was whether or not Tito was going to die.

At that time I remember being tormented by a song that my daughter kept playing on the gramophone. It was called 'Roxanne' and it was by some man who sang in a sort of falsetto voice, and it was all about how she didn't have to put on her red light, and it made me think about Roza saying that she used to charge five hundred pounds, and I was wondering how many men she'd had sex with. It made me feel repelled by her, without actually being repelled enough to stop wanting her. To be honest, the thought of it was also arousing. I don't know why, because it shouldn't have been. It was perverse. Maybe it was because I thought it increased the chances that she'd sleep with me. I still feel ashamed of having been like that.

My daughter was beginning to be very concerned about my interest in the music she was playing. It didn't seem right to her at all. It made her question her own good taste. I said to her, 'So, the whole point of it is to exclude your parents?' and she laughed, but didn't deny it.

When I called round, the BDU was wearing a black armband again, because of Mrs Thatcher. I looked at him and I thought, 'I'll give you ten years and you'll be voting Conservative just like your mummy and daddy. And then ten years after that you'll be admitting it, and ten years after that you'll be out canvassing for them.' Of course I didn't say anything. There's no point in patronising the young; you've just got to wait for them to become whatever they were always eventually bound to be.

Roza was in the basement in her usual greasy old armchair by the gas fire, and I was astonished to see that she had the BDU's cat on her lap, and she was combing it. It was a black-and-white fluffy animal with yellow eyes and a pointed nose, and it was kneading its paws and purring like an old Mercedes. I said, 'Roza, I thought you had a phobia about those things!' and she just smiled and said, 'So did I, but this one's nice. It waits for me and rubs against my legs when I get in, and at night it wants to come in and sleep with me. I'm not getting a pet bird this time, though.'

I said, 'Well, I'm amazed.'

'Things change,' she said. 'In the end everything changes, everything.' She smiled at me in a way that I can only describe as suggestive.

I sat down while she made me coffee and looked at

the cracks in the walls. They were getting bigger every time I visited. I wondered when they'd get round to demolishing the place and rebuilding it.

She came in and put the coffee down, and said, 'I was telling you about Francis and the boat.'

'So you were,' I said.

'He was nice,' said Roza. 'You know he had something sad about him. He made me feel like a mother.'

'Maternal is the word.'

'OK, maternal. Anyway, he was good with the boat. Always busy, always checking things. Always looking ahead at the sea. I was thinking, "Sure, he only took me on board because he wanted to screw me," but he wasn't doing anything about it. Sometimes he touched me, as if it was an accident, and I thought maybe it was and maybe not. I thought, "Maybe these English are just very polite or something."

'Anyway, one day he asked me, "Why are you leaving home?" and I told him lots of things, and then finally I told him about Alex, and I started to cry, maybe a little bit on purpose, maybe not, and we were sitting side by side in the galley, and he felt sorry for me and put his arm round me, and he said, "Hey, Roza, everyone's had a broken heart. It's not a good enough reason to leave home."

'Because he was kind to me, it made me cry properly, and he was giving me his handkerchief and all that, and I put my head on his chest and my hand went inside his shirt. It was an accident, but he thought it wasn't.'

I said, 'And where was the Australian?'

She said, 'He was out shopping. We were in the harbour at Rimini. It was very romantic.

'I said to him, "Sometimes I wish I was someone else," and he said something nice about liking me as I am. It made me feel warm inside. You know, and then we started kissing, and it all happened after that. Once he said he had the same problem, being tired and bored with himself. I thought, "No, it's impossible, you're rich and young and good-looking, and you don't even have to work," but now I know that everyone's escaping from themselves. Everybody's on the run, and then one day you've stopped running, and that's when you're dead, and nobody ever gets to be where they wanted. Don't you think so?'

I said, 'How come he had so much money?'

'Bubblegum.'

'Bubblegum?'

'You know, stupid songs for stupid bands of pretty boys and pretty girls. They get one big success, and then, phoo, you've never heard of them again. Francis said it was called bubblegum. That's why he got depressed sometimes. He had a big talent for composing crap songs. It makes you rich and also embarrassed. Maybe like being a good whore. Anyway, I said, "Why don't you write a book?" and he said, "Well, one day when I think of a story." I said, "You can put me in it," and he laughed. I said, "You know what? This boat, it's like the Young Communist Pioneer Camp. You get up early, and you do lots of compulsory activities." He thought that was good. I think maybe he fell in love with me because I said stupid things to make him laugh a little.

'I tell you what, I never worked so hard. My skin went all dark, and all my fat came off. I got so healthy it was like being drunk, very nice. I saw dolphins and porpoises, and there were birds that stopped and rested on the wires, and my mouth, it always had the nice taste of salt, and all my fingernails broke because of the work with the ropes, and my hair even got blonde bits when it was black before.

'Francis wanted to make the journey as long as possible, because he was in love with me and he was liking the fucking. We stopped everywhere. He wanted to show me lots of nice things. You know, it's fantastic how fast you can go with sails up. And when the wind doesn't work, you go with engines. A new harbour every evening! It was so romantic. My passport got full of stamps. What was boring was always being searched for drugs, you know, dogs on the boat and all that stuff. I felt guilty and I'd never even seen drugs before in my life.

'I liked Bonifacio. Alicante was OK. On Gibraltar there was an ape that tried to take my handbag. Those apes, they're like bloody Albanians for thieving. Portugal was nice; Figueira da Foz, Matozinhos. I never ate so much fish. And everywhere everybody knew Francis, the customs men and the fishermen and the taverna people, and everyone let us use their shower because the one on the boat was shit.

'I did fishing too. I got put off mullet because in the harbour when you flush the toilet on the boat, the mullet eat the shit. They wait by the toilet hole, and you see the water boiling because of them competing for it. I thought, "Bloody hell, no more mullet for Roza. I'm not eating fish that's made itself out of shit," but sometimes we stopped the boat and we caught nice fish. I caught the ugliest fish in the world, and it had big horrible eyes and it was all funny-shaped and with spines. I said, "I'm not eating that," but it was very nice.

'You know everything on a boat is called by another name? Like wall is bulwark and kitchen is galley, and left is port, and behind is aft, and you have special words for knots and everything on the boat. Once I remembered them but now I forget, unfortunately.'

'Weren't you seasick?'

'Oh shit, I was sick in the Bay of Biscay. It was the nasty sea. Storms and rocks and wrecks. We used the engines, no sails. Francis listened to the weather reports on the radio. He was always drawing lines on the maps, you know? Those waves were like hills, all coming from different places, and you had to try to face into them if you had the time to turn. If I was on deck I got freezing wet, if I was down below I got sick. I had a long wire with a clip and I was always attached to something, because of the waves. And it was raining, raining, raining, and the wind was sharp like glass.

'We stopped at Arcachon and looked at the biggest sand heap in Europe and ate some oysters, and they had little red squirrels in the pine trees, very pretty, and then we stopped at Brest and we did all our washing in a launderette, and we fell asleep in there while we waited, because of being so tired. We went in a hotel and had a proper bed and a proper shower, and we ate steak frites. It was the first night we never did any fucking, but it was OK again in the morning. And then in the English Channel the big problem was tankers. They spoiled it because you were always watching out, they didn't give you any peace. They were like whales, and you were feeling like the smallest little fish in the world.

'You know what? Everywhere I went, I sent a postcard to Alex, and on every one I said, "*Dear Bastard, I am very glad you are not here.*" It was very bad. I sent proper cards to Mama and my daddy and Tasha and Fatima. I kept thinking, "I can't believe I ever wanted to marry Alex."'

I interrupted her: 'Does that mean that now you wanted to marry Francis?'

'I was thinking about it. About what I'd say maybe, if he asked me. Anyway, it didn't work out. You know, one day I was watching the dolphins, and they were crossing the front of the boat and having a big game, and I said to Francis, "Why are they always so happy?" and he said, "It's because all that swimming makes you incredibly fit, and when you're incredibly fit you feel glad to have a body, and you just throw yourself around a lot." On the boat I was happy like a dolphin. Sometimes when I think about how everything got fucked up, I think, "It's OK, Roza, once you were happy like a dolphin." It's nice, thinking that I did manage it once.

'Francis said that in Corfu they've got stories about dolphins rescuing sailors from the sea, and if you kill one, even by mistake, it's one hundred and fifty years of bad luck. You know, I had big bad luck after Francis, and I never even killed a dolphin.'

21

Getting In

If I didn't love you so much, it wouldn't bother me.

Next time that Chris came round I was feeling a bit sad because I had just heard on the radio that John Wayne was dead. I'd been listening to that *Deer Hunter* tune, which I liked back then, and the news came on. I used to watch all those stupid westerns in the afternoons before I went back to the hostess club, and my head was still spinning with last night's champagne and cigarettes.

Because I was sad, I gave Chris an extra big hug when he came in, and he was very pleased. It made him all smiley. I told him about John Wayne, and he said 'I always liked James Stewart really. *Destry Rides Again*; what a great film!'

'I never saw it,' I said. Years later I did see it, and I enjoyed it a lot. It had a kind of sweetness.

Once I'd got him a coffee and we were sitting in the basement, and I'd lit up, Chris said, 'You know, it makes me very anxious, the amount of smoking that you do. It's like watching somebody committing suicide.'

'I started smoking big in the hostess club,' I said. 'You drink and smoke a lot. I only smoked a bit before then.'

'Last time I left here to see Dr Patel, he asked me if I'd started smoking, because I smelled of it.'

I just looked at him, and he said, 'It wouldn't matter if I wasn't fond of you. If I didn't like you so much, it wouldn't bother me, you committing suicide.'

I had the impression that he had been about to use the word 'love' but changed to 'like' at the last second. It made my heart jump. Chris said, 'I had an uncle who was a big smoker. He was a strong man, very well built, he'd been a boxing champion in the army. He smoked a lot, and then quite suddenly his lungs packed up, emphysema, you know. Because he couldn't breathe, his body wasted away, and he could hardly do anything at all. Once I was round there, and I had to help lift him off the toilet. He weighed almost nothing, and his hip bones were sticking through the skin. He had plasters over them. Do you know what he did?' Chris paused for the effect. 'One day he put a shotgun under his chin and blew the top of his head away. Brains and bones and hair all over the walls and ceiling. I was in the house at the time. It was the worst experience of my life, going into that room and seeing that horrible mess after we heard the shot and ran upstairs. My aunt lost her marbles straight away and died a few months later, mostly from the shock, in my opinion. That's why I want to shoot everyone in the tobacco trade. They're worse than Hitler. Just think how many millions they must have killed.' Chris looked at me very coolly, and I looked at my cigarette. I stubbed it out, even though it was only half smoked. The heap of butts in the tray suddenly looked horrible to me. He said, 'You were going to tell me about getting into the country.'

'Well,' I said, 'it was quite something when you look back, but it annoyed Francis a hell of a lot. It was the first time that I'd really pissed him off, and it made me feel like shit.

'We were in the Channel, and he said, "I think we should take you to Dover. It's a proper port of entry, and they'll have all the people there who can process your papers."

'I'd been dreading getting to this point. I said something stupid like, "Oh that was a musical sentence," and he raised an eyebrow, and I said, "Proper port of entry, people process papers," everything begins with a p.

'He laughed and said, "Yes, but what about entering at Dover?"

'You know, I took a great big breath, and I had a dread in my stomach, and I said, "I don't think I have the papers."

'He looked at me like I was a complete idiot. He said, "You don't have the papers? What do you mean, you don't have the papers? You told me you didn't need a visa. Is this a joke or something?"

'I was very embarrassed, I was sweating and my face was burning. I said, "I was afraid you wouldn't take me." He shouted at me, "Damn right I wouldn't have!" His eyes were glowing and fiery, and I felt like an insect. He'd never raised his voice to me before, and it was shocking.

'So I did what I had to do, and I started to cry. I was saying, "But I wanted to be in England," and he was saying, "Well, you bloody well can't be, can you?" and I was saying, "But please, I want to be in England."

'"I'm going to take you in and hand you over," he said, "and they can bloody well deport you if they want to. What the fuck did you think you were doing? Do you think I'm going to sail you back to Dubrovnik or something? How the fuck can you be so fucking stupid?"

'It was the first time I ever heard Francis use any bad words, and it made me feel very frightened. I was crying and saying, "Don't leave me, don't leave me." He was saying, "I could be fined! I could lose my boat! They could put me in prison for all I know! Jesus Christ! I thought I could trust you!"

'"Look," I said, "we got in everywhere else."

'"They were tiny places where the harbourmasters know me, and people like to visit for a couple of days. England is where every bloody foreigner wants to live, for some reason."

'I said, "Everyone speaks English." He glared at me, and I said, "Can't you ask someone if I need a visa?"

'"You expect me to radio the coastguard and ask how to get a Yugoslav into the country? You're madder than I thought."

'"Can't you radio someone else?"

'"Who, exactly? Do you think my mother has a radio set?"

'"OK," I said. "My head is made of shit. Mad bloody people from the Balkan." Then I said, "England's big, yes?"

'"Pretty big," he replied, and he was looking at me suspiciously.

'I said, "Lots of places for a boat to land?"

'He said, "No. Absolutely not. We'll just have to get into port and sort out the mess from there. We can find a consul or something."

'I was looking at him, horrified, and he said, "And that's that."

'I said, "I thought you loved me."

'He looked a bit like I'd hit him with a pan, and there was a very long silence while we just stared at each other, and he was wondering what on earth to say, and then finally he came up with: "You should wait for it to be said."

'I was looking at him very hard, and I said, "You've been fucking me like you loved me," and he replied, "You should still wait for it to be said."

'"Why?"

'"Because if you push it, it rolls over the edge and it gets broken."

'I got angry. I don't know why. Maybe I didn't know what else to do, and I could see all my plans going down the toilet, and all my hopes messed up. I got so angry I started kicking the cabin door, and I was shouting, "Bloody English! Bloody English! Bloody fucking English!" and then I did some shouting in Serbo-Croat, and I got a cooking knife and I stuck it into the wood, and I went and I started looking for things to throw in the sea, and I threw in a plate and the kettle, but then he came and held onto my wrists, and he was very strong, much stronger than I expected, and I kept kicking him in the legs but he wouldn't move, and he just held my wrists until I ran out of energy, and I started crying again. We could see the white cliffs, and I remembered my daddy saying he'd always wanted to see them, and I was thinking that he never would, and that just made me cry even more. I was leaning over the guard rail and thinking about jumping in the sea and giving up on this stupid world.

'Francis let the sails go slack, so the boat was just

tossing and crashing about on the water. I always hated it when he did that. He came up to me and said, "Look, it isn't that I don't want to break the law. It's that I don't want to get caught. Personally, I think people like you ought to be recruited, not kept out. But if I get caught, I've got a criminal record, and I don't know what the penalty is."

'I said, "OK, take me to France and leave me somewhere. I don't care any more."

'He tightened up the sails again, and we started going quite fast. We went past the North Foreland, and I was wondering what was going to happen to me. There were lots of big ships to avoid, because it was the Thames Estuary coming up. I said, "Are you going to take me to London?" and he said, "You must be fucking joking."

It turned out that he'd decided to go home by the usual route, because that wasn't suspicious. It was just a question of talking to the usual people on the radio and doing the normal things.

'Just past Felixstowe we dropped anchor and waited for the tide to come in, because there were sandbanks that kept moving about, and he told me what the plan was. I packed up my things, and then I looked at the boat and all the familiar things about it, and I began to feel nostalgic already. All the nice shiny brass and wooden things. I thought, "OK, one day I'm going to marry Francis and I'll be a British citizen, and then I'll come back to this boat and we'll go off to the sea again." I thought, "OK, so I don't love him too much, the way I loved Alex, but I like him anyway, and the sex is bloody good, and we get on like friends, so why not? I bet he'd be a good father."

'We were coming down the Orwell Estuary, and he sailed very close to one bank, just using the engines, you know? We stopped and he dropped the anchor, and we lowered down the little dinghy, and it was going up and down and scraping against the side of the *Sweet Olivia Bunbury*, so that I was worried about the varnish.

'He went down the little ladder, and then he held on while I climbed down. He said, "Have you any idea how bloody stupid this is?" as I stepped into the dinghy. He had a rope tied up to the *Sweet Olivia*, and as we rowed to the shore he just let it coil out of the boat. It was only forty metres but it seemed a very long way.

'We landed on a concrete slope covered with that slippery green weed that's like silk. There was a little yard of derelict boats in a patch of woods. There was a great big iron hull, upside down, and it was rusted through, and it was up on blocks. Francis said, "If it rains while you're waiting, just nip under there." It must have been a very elegant boat in its great days.

'He gave me a little kiss on the cheek, and he hauled himself back to the *Sweet Olivia Bunbury*. I watched him climb up on deck, raise the anchor and press the starter. He gave me a little wave, and off he went to Ipswich.

'I waited there for two hours. I had all the usual panics: "Maybe he's just abandoned me, maybe he had a heart attack, maybe he crashed, maybe he went to the police." I sat in the woods by the river, with all those abandoned boats rotting around me, and I thought about how everything falls to bits in the end. Anyway, Francis did finally come in his car and pick me up. He'd cleared customs and put the boat to bed. That's what he called it, "putting the boat to bed". When he walked down into the wood I was so pleased to see him that I cried.'

Chris listened to what I said and then asked, 'So where did you go?'

'Oh, Francis had a house near Ipswich. It was a nice house in a village called Bentley. There was a pub called the Case is Altered. I always remembered that. It was such a funny name. The village was OK. I sort of liked it, but it wasn't very exciting. It was a place for being peaceful. I stayed with Francis for two years.'

'What happened?'

'It was me. My own stupid fucking fault as usual. I got fed up.'

'Fed up?'

'You know, being in the same place, sleeping with the same man that I didn't love too much, too much trouble to get into Ipswich on the bloody bus and back again, no bloody job, always eating the same meals and saying the same things. I was a shithead, like always.'

'At least you know you're a shithead,' said Chris. 'I am, but I don't know it yet. Not Know with a big K. I get a lot of hints that I ignore.'

'It was a good time for Francis, though. You know, he loved me, and it made him write good bubblegum. The next year we went out in the boat again, for three months, and I got out and back in the same way. We laughed about it and it didn't bother us. Really it was all good adventures.'

'But you finished it?'

'I finished it. I wanted more interesting things. You know, London, Buckingham Palace, British Museum, intellectuals talking about big things, the Underground, the theatre, rich people in nice cars, a big affair with someone fantastic, like Mick Jagger, maybe Prince Charles. Francis didn't want me to go, and he cried a lot and he even begged me, and he told me he loved me and he wanted to marry me. But, you know me, I was full of shit and I didn't realise till it was too late. I couldn't get it out of my mind for years, how I fucked it all up and hurt him, and how I had stupid ideas about love. You know, he even helped me find a room in London, and he paid the deposit, and he gave me six hundred pounds just to get me started. He did that even though I kicked him in the belly.'

Chris said, 'But wouldn't he have had you back?'

'Maybe, but when I finally got back in touch with him he'd got married, and he was happy anyway. He said, "Roza, I really loved you." If I'd got in touch a year before, maybe everything would have worked out, but I didn't think he'd want me. I didn't feel good enough to ask. I was just a piece of crap by then. That's what I thought, after what happened. I wouldn't be able to accept anyone who was stupid enough to accept me. I could have just telephoned, but every time I went to a telephone box, I just picked up the receiver and then put it back down again, and thought, "Maybe I'll call tomorrow," and sometimes I went in and out of the box, lifting the receiver and putting it down again, and then someone else would come and want to use the phone, and I'd go away and wait another day.'

'I've often done things like that,' said Chris. Then he asked, 'So why weren't you good enough?'

'Well, you know what I did. Why would he want me? I was a bloody prostitute.'

Chris said, 'He never would have found out if you didn't tell him.'

Chris and I sat there in silence for a while, and then I said, 'You know what? When we were driving from the place where I landed, I saw the most beautiful bridge over the river. It was all white and graceful like a swan, and it made me happy just to see it. You know how green everything is in England? And all the foreigners say, "Oh, England is so green." But what I noticed was the white bridge over the river.'

'That must be the Orwell Bridge,' said Chris.

'I'd love to see it again one day,' I said. 'When I saw it the first time, it made me think that England must be a great country to live in.'

22

Bergonzi's Pussycat Hostess Paradise

You get some right dodgy sods around here.

Chris came back a couple of weeks later, standing on the doorstep and rubbing his hands, saying, 'Well, well, that's the end of an era, eh?'

'What is?'

'Oh, you know, Muhammad Ali packing it in. He's retiring. And I remember when he beat Sonny Liston. Isn't it incredible how the time goes?'

'Boxing is stupid,' I said.

'All the same, he's the most famous person in the world.'

'No one's more famous than the Queen,' I said, 'and she's not packing it in.'

'She'll be there forever, unless the IRA get her first. Anyway, am I allowed in?'

We went down in the basement, and I made him some tea. He was drinking it Continental-style by now, because I said that putting milk in it was a stupid British custom that no one in the rest of the world could see the sense of, and if you didn't make it so strong you wouldn't have to put anything in it, unless you liked lemon. Anyway, he tried it, and said it wasn't bad, and after that he became converted, so I thought maybe the British aren't doomed to bad gastronomy forever. Chris said that the Irish drink it even stronger and milkier than the British. I saw an Irish cookbook once, and it was about three millimetres thick.

I knew it was going to be awkward today because we'd got to the point of talking about the hostess club. I was sure we were about to become lovers, and I didn't want to put him off, but it was too late to change the story now because I'd already mentioned too many details already.

The Bob Dylan Upstairs was learning *The Deer Hunter*, and you could hear the tune coming down the staircase, along with all the mistakes and the places where he stopped. He was learning the version for classical guitar, like in the film, because he said it was better than the electric version that was the latest hit. I was getting to like him quite a lot. We were doing a lot of talking just as I did with Chris. I was doing so much talking that I wondered if I'd ever stop. I wondered if it was a kind of sickness in me. I wondered why people didn't get bored with me. I thought, 'One day I've got to stop talking, and start living.' I was thinking all the time that I wanted to be with Chris, even if I was only a mistress. It wouldn't have bothered me. I never met his wife, but it was obvious that there was nothing to be jealous of. He called her 'The Great White Loaf', which was cruel, but funny. I would have liked all the time to myself that you get if you're a mistress. I wanted him around me, that's all. When we were talking, I kept having this urge to get up and give him a hug, and kiss him on the neck. I didn't though. Now I think that I should have.

'So what's next?' he asked, when we were sitting down, even though he knew perfectly well what was next.

'Bergonzi's Pussycat Hostess Paradise,' I said.

'Is that what it was called? The brothel?'

I was offended. 'It wasn't a brothel, it was a hostess club.'

'Never been to one,' said Chris. 'I don't really know what they are.'

'I didn't either. But I got a job working in a bar. It was a pub really. It's difficult to get decent work when you're illegal. You end up in bars and cafés, and businesses belonging to Pakistanis and Greek Cypriots and people like that who don't give a damn about the law. Or rich people who want a nice girl to look after the children and do some cleaning, that's another one.

'Anyway, I was in the pub in Clapham behind the bar, and a man started talking to me when I was in between getting drinks. He was nice. He had a gold tiepin and a big gold ring on his finger. He said, "A good-looking girl like you's wasting her time in a place like this. I bet you don't earn much, do you, darling?" I said it wasn't too bad, and he said, "Well, you could be earning a couple of hundred a night, and that's without doing anything, almost."

'I said, "What's that then?" and he said, "Hostess club. Mate of mine runs one. What the girls earn in there, well, you just wouldn't believe it. All you got to do is be nice to the blokes who turn up looking for a break from their old ladies."

'I got the wrong idea straight away, and I said, "You

think I want to be a prostitute? If you think I want to be a prossie you can just piss off." I was picking up the London way of talking, see?

'Anyway, he laughed at me, and he said, "No, no, no. What happens is, they come in and you chat to them, right? You take an interest in them, right? Then they buy champagne. That's your job. You get them to buy champagne, right? And you get commission on each bottle. Those geezers cough up a fuckin' fortune for each bottle, excuse my French, and you get a percentage, and you get paid right before you go home, on the nail. You wouldn't believe it, but some blokes don't mind paying hundreds for a bottle of bubbly."

'"They must be stupid," I said, and he said, "Nah, not really, they're just stinking rich or bleedin' lonely, and usually both."

'He ordered another pint, and said, "Are you interested, then?"

'I said, "It's not one of those places where they get men to come in and then give them lots of drinks, and then give them a huge bill at the end? I heard about how they catch foreigners like that. People who don't understand pounds."

'"No, love, that's a clip joint. This is a hostess club. It's different. There is one drawback, though."

'"Oh, yes?" I said. "So what's that?" and he replied, "You've got to dress up like a bleedin' pussycat."

'"A pussycat?"

'"Yeah, a bleedin' pussycat. You know, tail and ears and whiskers, and all that, and black fishnet stockings and stilettos."

'I said, "Do cats wear stilettos and stockings, then?" and he said, "London ones do, darling. You mean you 'aven't noticed?"

'Anyway, he gave me an address in Soho, and he put a little message with it, and he said, "Don't bother going before five o'clock." I thought, "What the hell, there's no harm in taking a look."

'Anyway, Bergonzi's Pussycat Hostess Paradise Club was up some stairs from the street, and it was pretty bad to look at until you turned down the ordinary lights and put on the coloured ones. It was almost like this house, but not so bad. Everything dirty and old. But with red lights it looked like luxury. It was just a big bar, really, with little low glass-topped tables and lots of sofas and armchairs, and red carpet and sheepskins that weren't really sheep, but something fake that you could put in the washing machine. It smelled stale because no one ever opened the windows.

'When I got there, I went up the stairs and at the top there was a door with a grille in it, and I knocked, and this man looked through at me and said, "Sod off."

'I said, "I've come to see Bergonzi. Bob sent me."

'So he let me in, and he turned out to be a giant man in a bow tie who looked like a gorilla, and that's what everyone called him, and he didn't even mind. They just said, "Hi, Grill, how are you, Grill?" and he was all right really. He never said much, he just got rid of shitty customers. I never had much to do with him. He had a hobby collecting exotic empty cigarette packets that got left by foreign customers. Everyone said his flat was full of them. Anyway, Grill let me in when I said I'd come to see Bergonzi. That's when I saw how depressing the place was with the ordinary lights on. Even so, it had a little pool with a fountain in the middle, and lots of plastic plants, and big bits of velvety cloth draped all over the place.

'Bergonzi was all right. He was Italian cockney. That's what he said, anyway. He looked like a bloody mafioso; you know, white shoes, black shirt and trousers, big suntan, sunglasses like you don't need indoors, nice white teeth.

'Bergonzi looked at me and said, "Well, doll, you're tasty." I gave him the little note from Bob, and he read it and said, "Good old Bob. Trouble is, if I take you on, it means I owe 'im a monkey."

'I couldn't believe it. "A monkey?"

'"Commission. Don't know the lingo, eh?" he said, and then, "Do you know how this place runs? Cos if you don't know, and then you don't like it, we'll all have been wasting our time, won't we?"'

I asked Chris, 'Do you want to see my imitation of Bergonzi? All the girls had one.' Chris said, 'OK,' so I got myself ready. I stood up and puffed out my chest a bit, and kept pushing the imaginary sunglasses up on my nose. Then I began:

'"Right, doll, it's like this, it's dead simple, like fallin' off a log. We gotta lotta rich geezers comin' in 'ere wiv more dosh than common sense. All yer gotta do is be nice to 'em, right? Chat 'em up, use your powers, get 'em to buy champagne. Cos that's the secret. A bottle a champagne costs the punters ninety quid a throw, and I pay you thirty quid for each bottle the punter knocks back, right? So you're my little salesman.

'"Here's the club rules. Number one, admission by

membership only, annual membership five hundred quid, but you can join for one night for fifty if you're that stupid and that loaded.

'"Here's the rules for the girls. Number one: no bleedin' taxman, no national insurance, payment cash-in-'and only. Rule number two: no bleedin' 'anky-panky on the premises. If you want a bit of extramarital that's down to you, some of the girls do and some of them don't. I got birds here earnin' a couple ton a night, catch my drift? But you go to a bleedin' hotel or something. I don't wanna know. I don't want the filth up 'ere chargin' me for bein' a ponce or something.

'"Rule number next: drink as much champers as you can 'old, and pour the rest down the plants when the punter goes to the lavvy. Rule number whatever: strictly don't get pissed, cos it's embarrassing, and that's how you get fired. You gotta wear our little uniform. We give you one, but you go out and get your black tights and your high heels all on your own, and make sure they make yer arse wiggle, nice and sexy. Rule number wotsit: if yer gonna smoke, smoke classy ones, nice and long, white filters, dinky little gold band. No Woodbines, and strictly no bleedin' roll-ups."'

I sat down again, and Chris said, 'You should have been an actress; that was pretty good.'

'Anyway,' I said, 'Bergonzi gave me ten pounds to go out and buy the shoes and stockings, and he didn't even know me. He was nice, really. He said, "Thank God for Bob, because the girls keep buggering off and marrying the bloody customers."

'I nearly didn't go back. I thought maybe it was bad work for someone like me. You know, I should be in a university somewhere, not in a shitty club dressed up like a cat. It was . . . how do you say it?'

'Demeaning? Beneath you?'

'Yes, beneath me. It was just a stupid job, you know, nothing important, but I thought, "OK, it's plenty of money, and I don't have to stay long, and it's a good way to practise English."

'Next morning I went to Oxford Street, and I bought shoes and stockings, and I looked at all the shops with nice things in, and I thought, "Lucky Roza, you can buy these things before too long." I went and looked at Leicester Square and Piccadilly, and I looked in the bookshops on Charing Cross Road. I was killing time, as you say. And I had a pizza, and I saw a man who had a big board, and on the board it said that you shouldn't eat meat because the protein makes you lustful, and if you're lustful you go to hell. I followed him around a bit because I thought, "I never saw anyone like him in Yugoslavia." I looked at the pigeons in Trafalgar Square, and I listened to some people playing violin and guitar together at St Martin's, on the steps, and then a bloody policeman came and told them to go away, and everyone who'd been listening started shouting at the policeman and telling him to piss off, and I enjoyed that. In Yugoslavia no one tells the police to piss off. Then I got my portrait done by a hippy person who was working on the pavement by the National Gallery, and he made me look like a film star or something. It was nice, I killed a whole day.

'I went to the club at half past nine, and Grill let me in. Bergonzi came and said hello, and he introduced me to a thin woman with red hair called Val, and this Val said she was manageress and she looked after all the girls. After a while I realised that Bergonzi and Val were having an affair, and his wife didn't know.

'Val was nice. She helped me put on the pussycat suit, and I looked in the mirror and I didn't know whether to laugh or be angry. I said to Val, "I don't think I want to do this."

'She said, "Bloody ridiculous, innit, love? If I was you I'd just have a good laugh about it. There's worse things; you could be shagging lepers in the Congo or cleaning bogs in China."

'I said, "I feel stupid," and she said, "It ain't you wot's stupid, it's the bleedin' punters who get a kick out of it. What you 'ave to do is say, 'It's them that's daft, and me wot's making idiots out of them by lifting their cash.' Simple really."

'I said, "I still don't think I can do it," and Val said, "Well, just try it once. If you can't stand it, don't come back. Shall we do the make-up?" And I ended up with great big pussycat eyes, and these whiskers glued to my face.'

Chris laughed and said, 'You must have looked very sweet really,' and I said, 'You know what? I got to like that pussycat suit. Mine was black with a white front, and it had a sort of hood with ears on, so you only saw my face. It was quite comfortable really. I had to wear white gloves.'

'I dressed my daughter up as a squirrel once,' said Chris. 'It was for a fancy dress party. She looked so adorable that I almost couldn't stand it.'

'She probably wasn't in her twenties,' I said. 'Anyway, after a while I realised what the real advantage of the suit was.'

'Oh yes?'

'It was a good disguise. You could be anyone you wanted dressed up like that. You could talk any old shit to the punters. When you changed back into your normal clothes, it was like washing your hands. You went home with a clean mind and you were normal again. I liked that. The only thing I never liked was those stilettos. You know, I had sore feet all the time and they never got better till I left.'

'What were the other girls like?' asked Chris.

'Not too young, but not old either. They were all shiny, as if they polished themselves a lot. A bit too thin. Lots of foreigners like me. Two of them were junkies and it was how they got enough money without being prostitutes. They had awful scars on their arms, so it was lucky about the pussycat suits. A lot were fucking the customers for money. One of them was married and her husband made her do it so he could stay at home and watch football. A lot of them had children and no husband, and they had to get home so they could get the children up and take them to school, and then they came home again and went to bed. You know, they all fell down somehow, and didn't know how to get back up. I heard sad stories, sad stories all the time. I was the only one with no sad story. You know, God didn't shit on me yet. He was just waiting, I found out. Some of them were clever like me, and some of them had no brain at all. A lot of them didn't stay. I'd get to know them, and then they'd leave. I don't have any friends left out of all those girls. They were like birds with broken wings, and they stayed while they waited for the wings to get repaired, and then they flew away.'

'What about the men? What were the men like?'

'The men? OK, thirty-five to sixty years old. Rich. Frigid shitty wives, if you believe them. They drank too much. They told you unbelievable secret things, like you were the best friend or the psychiatrist. The nice ones, they came often, and when they saw you they gave a little kiss on the cheek, and you got fond of them, and that's how a lot of the girls got away. The bad ones, you know, there were some bad ones who got too drunk and they got loud and wanted to fight or put their hands up your pussycat suit, and if it got too bad, the Grill just threw them out and threw their entrance money down the stairs after them. Normally you could get them so drunk that they got ill, and that was the best revenge. Sometimes you got gangsters, and you couldn't get the Grill to throw them out because they might send someone to bomb the club, so Val put something in their drink, and they'd wake up on the floor in the morning and not remember anything.

'Everything was fine, you know. I worked six months and I had some nice conversations and some stupid ones, and I smoked too much and drank champagne, and I liked the girls, and Val and Bergonzi, and lots of the regulars. It was a little family. No, it was a big family, you know, the kind of family with lots of cousins who keep coming round, like bloody Greeks. It was a weird life, Chris. I never saw daylight, hardly. I was eating nothing but rubbish, crisps and sandwiches and things, and I was sleeping all day. I forgot about trees and the sun. I laughed a lot, but I never had anything to remember, every day the same but just a bit different. I don't remember anything. I got so much money, so much money, and I never got to the shops to spend it. Then the Big Bastard came in.'

'The Big Bastard?'

'The Big Bastard.'

'So, what happened?'

'He was this big guy, lots of money. He never said what he did. He said "international businessman". He never came before. Bergonzi didn't know him. He paid a year's membership straight away, five hundred pounds. He was all pleased with himself, that's for sure. He walked in like he was Mussolini or something, like he just won the Nobel Prize for being a hotshot.

'He came to my table and he interrupted me when I was talking to someone, and he said, "Hey, pussycat." He had a funny accent, I don't know if he was American or South African or English from somewhere I didn't know about. He sat down next to me, and the man I was talking to looked very surprised, but in the end he just got up and went and talked to a Bulgarian girl. The Big Bastard said, "So where are you from?" and I said, "Yugoslavia," and he said, "So where's that?" and I said, "It's a little place in the middle of France where everyone's a millionaire and no one pays tax." He said, "Well, I never knew that."

'He told me about his houses and his swimming pools in different shapes, and his two Bentley cars and a Daimler and a Rolls-Royce, and his chain of burger shops, and he told me about all these famous people he was personal friends with, and all the beautiful women he'd had and how they all wanted him back. Anyway, I just got him as drunk as I could, so he'd get ill. And he was smoking these big horrible cigars that Bergonzi was selling, and he still didn't get ill, and he just kept talking and putting his hands on me, and all the other girls were looking at me and making sympathetic faces, and finally it was two o'clock in the morning.

'I went for a pee, and I found Bergonzi and I said, "Look, I've really got to go home. I can't stand this man, and I don't feel good."

'He said, "Sorry, doll, but you don't leave till the punter does. That's how it is, that's the deal."

'I said, "Oh please, Gonzo," and he said, "No, I'm really sorry, love, but that's how it is."

'So it got to half past three and it was if I'd been in hell forever and ever, but then the Big Bastard said, "I expect you'd like to get home, eh, pussycat?" and I said, "Well, I am tired," and he said, "OK, me too. I'll be going myself." So he got his coat from the Grill, and he went. I went for another pee, and on the way out Bergonzi said, "OK, love, it's not busy now, you might as well go home," and he gave me the money for that night, which came to quite a lot. Just before I went Bergonzi said, "Mind how you go, you get some right dodgy sods around here." So I went down into the street, and that's when it happened.'

'What happened?'

'Look, Chris, it isn't easy, you know?'

'Well, you don't have to tell me.'

'I ought to tell someone, Chris. I never told anyone else, and it's a big thing. It's lots of big things.'

'Just tell me one thing, and maybe you'll tell me the next thing later.'

'OK, I went down to the street, and I was just smelling the air because it was all fresh and damp, even though it was Soho. It was raining when I was inside talking to the Big Bastard. I was thinking I'd get a taxi, because the nice thing was I could afford a taxi every night. I thought I'd find one in Leicester Square, no problem.

'I'd just started off when this big black limousine came along, and it slowed down, and it had two men in it. One was driving and the other was in the back, and it came right next to me, and this electric window came down, and it was the Big Bastard sitting in the back and waggling his fingers and his gold rings at me, and he said, "Hey, pussycat, guess who's coming for a ride." '

'Oh shit,' said Chris.

23
The Prison

She lost hope even though she was a partisan's daughter.

I'd finally saved the five hundred pounds. It was in its Manila envelope, in the breast pocket of my jacket. Every now and then I took it out and looked at it, avoiding the temptation to count the money again. I'd done that several times, and used up a number of envelopes. It was certainly five hundred pounds. It gave me an odd sense of reassurance. Theoretically I now had enough money to go to bed with Roza, if she had still been doing that sort of thing.

It occurred to me that I could go and spend it on some other woman from somewhere like Bergonzi's Pussycat Hostess Paradise, but I knew straight away that it wasn't what I wanted, no matter how lonely and sex-starved I was. After so many years of that marriage to the Great White Loaf, I didn't think that I had any attractions to make a woman want me, my mouth was full of dust, and I didn't have any confidence, but even so, my dreams had settled on Roza. I knew that she was fond of me, but I wasn't sure what kind of fondness it was. I was frightened to broach the subject in case her affection was of the kind that the girls of my youth would call 'platonic'. The disappointment would have been crushing.

At about this time, Roza told me of the worst experience of her life, about being abducted by the 'Big Bastard' and his accomplice.

The two men forced her into the car, and the man she called the 'Big Bastard' sat in the back with her, holding a knife in his hand. She thought that they drove her for at least two hours, but it was still just dark when they arrived somewhere and she was told to get out of the car.

They took her down some steps into a sort of furnished basement. It even had a shower and a lavatory, but no windows, and the door was locked at the top of the steps. It was the kind of door that had steel sheeting nailed to it. Roza said that she thought it had been specially adapted by the Big Bastard and his friend, precisely for this kind of thing, that they did it as a sort of hobby. She said that if you looked carefully, you could see places where bloodstains had been cleared up, and there were rips in the furniture. There was a light that you couldn't turn off unless you stood on a chair and unscrewed the bulb.

Roza said that she hadn't kicked or screamed or fought, because a kind of fatalism overcame her, a combination of fatalism and terror that makes you paralysed. I've never been in a situation like that. I like to think that I would put up a fight, but maybe I wouldn't. You never know till it happens to you, what your reaction will be. I remember I came across a blind rabbit once, on a walk in the country, and it knew I was standing over it, but it didn't know what I was. It was terrified but it couldn't do anything, so it just hunkered down in the grass at the side of the path. It laid its head down, straight ahead, just as the aristocrats lay their heads on the block in films about Elizabeth I, and waited for me to kill it. I stroked its nose and said soothing things, and then I picked it up and put it further from the path. It kicked when I was carrying it, but when I put it down it adopted the same attitude of waiting for execution. I suppose it was like that for Roza. She lost hope even though she was a partisan's daughter. She said she'd discovered that even atheists pray when they're desperate.

They kept her there for four days and fed her on sandwiches and chocolates with nuts in. They weren't just rapists. She showed me a burn on her upper arm the size of a shilling, and said, 'They didn't stub out cigarettes like a normal torturer; they stubbed out a cigar.'

Apart from the rapes and all the other sexual humiliations, they beat her and cut her, and even bit her. She had bruises on her neck like big fingerprints, because they liked to throttle her until she fell unconscious, and her wrists and ankles had red rings round them from when she had been tied down. She said she had injuries all over, but the abductors had paid special attention to hurting her in the places you'd expect. At that point I didn't want to hear any more details.

To begin with I had been listening to her in horror and consternation, but it rapidly got worse. I had such a sick feeling in my stomach that I stopped drinking the tea she'd made for me. Then I started to shake. She said, 'Chris, you're so pale, are you all right?'

I tried to speak, but it was impossible. I was thinking

about the horrible things that she had suffered, and it was breaking my heart.

It was the first time I'd cried since I'd arrived at the hospital and found that my brother had already died, and I was too late.

I had huge tears running down my face, and I couldn't stop them. I was holding the cup of tea in one hand, and some of the drops fell in it. I felt ridiculous, but I was overwhelmed.

Roza just looked at me for a few moments, and then stopped talking. She came over and put her arms around me, and that made me weep even more, as though the contact was the trigger to release all that agonising sympathy. She went round the back of the chair and put her face next to mine. I could feel her thick silky hair, and smell her familiar flowery scent, a combination of soap and face cream and perfume. I will always remember it, the wonderful feeling of her embracing me like a mother or a sister, her cheek against my cheek. I sometimes wonder whether she was crying too. Her face was wet, but the tears were probably mine. She squeezed me very tight and started to rock me a little bit. She was saying, 'Oh Chris, I'm sorry, I'm so sorry. Please, I'm so sorry.'

For ages after that I looked for literature about the psychological effects of rape. I wanted to understand what it might be like, being Roza. I mean, I had no idea.

The odd thing is that I found almost nothing, there was no information at all. I got in touch with a group called WAR, but they weren't much use. Being a man didn't help, and they probably thought I was a pervert.

One book I found eventually was by that girl who got raped in a vicarage. I read it twice, but I wasn't sure that it was any use to me, because Roza wasn't exactly a vicar's daughter.

24
After the Big Bastard

I used to wake up in the afternoon, and I was crying.

I felt very bad about Chris crying like that. I didn't think he would be so affected. I often cry out of sympathy, when I see the news of a disaster on the television, and sometimes I cry out of happiness, such as when I saw the wedding of Princess Anne, and when I heard that Juan Carlos had become King of Spain. It wasn't that I particularly like kings or anything, it was just that I was happy for them. Maybe I'm odd.

Before that, I'd never had anybody start crying inconsolably when I told them a sad story about myself, though. His tears made me feel very guilty and unworthy, and I even thought that perhaps there was something wrong with me because I don't think I would have cried like that in his situation. I was expecting him to get angry about the Big Bastard, to be outraged, but I never expected him to weep. I told the same story to the Bob Dylan Upstairs, once, and he just strode around the room swearing, saying that he'd like to tear that man's throat out, and cut his balls off and make him swallow them, and then eat the shit when he finally shat them out. It made me laugh because when I first knew him he told me he was a pacifist. But with Chris it ended up with me giving him hugs as if he were a little child, and sympathising with him for his sympathy with me. I even cried a bit myself.

He quietened down after a while and I made him a cup of tea, British-style for once, too strong, with milk and sugar in it. He drank the tea and felt a lot better, and I had to carry on giving him the story, with him looking at me all desolate, and me sitting there feeling like a criminal.

I told him that the Big Bastard and his friend had taken me back to Soho and turfed me out of the car at three in the morning. I couldn't think what else to do but to go to the Pussycat Paradise Hostess Club. The place was winding down but there were some people still there, and when I went up the stairs the Gorilla looked at my face and said, 'What the fuck happened to you?' It was the longest sentence he ever said to me, or to anyone else.

Bergonzi said, 'Bloody 'ell, doll, what happened to you?' and Val said almost exactly the same thing. Anyway, they gave me a bowl of crisps and a glass of champagne, and I told them about the Big Bastard and his friend. Val was very sweet to me, and she said, 'We was really worried about you, love.' Bergonzi said that sometimes you got people like that who preyed on girls from hostess clubs because they never went to the police afterwards. He said 'What did they look like, love?' and the odd thing was, I couldn't really remember. Everyone tried to remember the Big Bastard from when he'd originally come to the Pussycat Paradise, but you got too many people to remember them for more than a day or two. The odd thing was that the Gorilla did remember, and he actually drew quite a good picture. Val said, 'Bleedin' 'eck, who would have thought it? Grill's got talents. I ain't never gonna see 'im the same way now.' Bergonzi photocopied it and said he was going to send the pictures round to the other clubs. I don't know if anything came of it.

Chris said, 'So what did you do? You didn't stay at the club, did you?'

I said, 'I stayed. Val and Bergonzi let me stay in their secret flat with them for a few days, and Val looked after me really nicely. Even Bergonzi brought me trays of food, but it was the kind of thing you'd expect from a man. You know, a bit of cheese, and a bit of cake, and a bit of tinned ham, and an apple with wrinkles.'

Chris said, 'You wouldn't normally think of night-club owners being kind people,' and I said, 'You don't know any.'

Chris said, 'But why did you stay at the club, after what happened to you?' and I said, 'Because it was my family. I didn't have anyone else. They were the only people I knew, and they liked me and I liked them. It was a little world all on its own, that wasn't like any other world. I put on the pussycat suit, and smoked a lot, and drank champagne, and talked rubbish to men, and laughed with Val and the girls, and I could put off the world forever. You know, I washed myself a lot after that. I still can't stand cigars. I used to wake up in the afternoon, and I was crying. I got bad dreams, over and over, always the same bad dreams. I got woken up, so I had a couple of cigarettes, and then I'd go back to sleep. I still wash too much, maybe. Anyway, some other bad things happened, and Val helped me.'

‘Oh?’ said Chris.

‘Val took me to the VD clinic, and it wasn’t nice at all. It was a horrible place with tatty posters on the wall. Anyway, it was OK, I wasn’t infected, but it didn’t make me feel any better about it. Then it turned out I was pregnant.’

‘You were pregnant? Shit.’

‘Yes,’ I said. ‘You know, rapists don’t bother with johnnies.’

Chris said, ‘So what did you do?’ and I said, ‘Well, Val organised for me to get an abortion.’

Chris just said, ‘Oh God,’ and I said, ‘You know, one day, I am going to have a baby with a nice father, and I’ll hope it’s the same baby come back again, but this time the father will be nice, because I always felt bad about that baby.’

‘You’d be a good mother,’ said Chris. ‘The father would be lucky.’

I was very touched, and I held his hand for a moment. He said, ‘I don’t usually agree with abortion, but then you hear stories like these.’

I said, ‘Nobody wants to grow up a rapist’s child. It would be a curse. And what if it’s in his blood? Anyway, I was ill for ages afterwards.’

‘It wasn’t a backstreet abortion, was it?’

‘Oh no, Val organised a proper clinic and everything. They were nice to me and it was a clean place, and there were lots of girls there, all feeling sorry. But one day I started bleeding in the street. There was blood everywhere, all down my legs. That’s why I like black people, because it was a black man who went to a phone box and called an ambulance.’

Chris looked at me a little incredulously and said, 'You can't like a whole race just because one of them was nice to you.'

I said, 'Well, I hate Bosnians because one of them was horrible to me,' and he said, 'I think you should take bigger samples.' I knew he was right, but that's the way I am. I said, 'Don't you like black people?' and he said, 'I hardly know any. I only know Asians, because a lot of them become doctors, and they buy in pharmaceuticals.'

'Anyway,' I said, 'I got better after a while, and I was back at the club again, and then I started getting this idea that I wanted to kill the Big Bastard and the other man. I just couldn't get it out of my head. It was a big obsession.'

'I can understand that,' said Chris. 'Do you really have it in you to be a murderer, though?'

I said, 'Come on, you know what I am,' and he laughed and said, 'OK, you're a partisan's daughter.'

I looked at him and said, 'I'm serious. I wanted to kill them. I got some shoes that were too big, and long gloves up to my elbow, and a black dress, and I went to the market and I got a perfect knife.'

'A perfect knife?'

I bent down and picked up my handbag. I took the knife out and showed it to him. I said, 'Watch out, because it's the sharpest knife. I got it sharpened by this Cypriot cook that I got to know once. I never told you about him. Anyway, I said it was for meat.' It was a filleting knife, one of those nice Sabatier knives with the black handles and the rivets. Chris held it in his hand and looked at it, and I said, 'It's supposed to be sharp enough to shave with.' He tried it on the hairs on the back of his hand, and said, 'Christ, Roza, you really go everywhere with that? And you even made it a little sheath.' When he gave it back he said, 'I must remember to stay on the right side of you. I don't suppose you ever used it?'

I hesitated. I was very tempted to say yes. I mean, what fun it would be if I told Chris I was a murderer. But I said, 'He never came back to the club. I thought maybe if he came back I could get him drunk and take him to some place like under an arch at King's Cross, or maybe an empty warehouse in Deptford or something. I was going to say that we were going to my place, and I was going to make him scream with pleasure, and things like that. Anyway, my father said you should never stick a knife through someone's ribs because the ribs are like springs, and you can't pull the knife out again. I was going to get him under the ribs, and stick it up through his heart, like this.' I showed him how I was going to swing it up from underneath.

'Do you still want to kill him?'

'It's just a little dream,' I said. 'I expect somebody else has killed him by now.'

'I'm very sorry about what happened to you,' Chris said, and I could see that his eyes were wet again.

'You know what?' I said. 'When I got back to the Pussycat Paradise after all that, and I looked in my handbag, I found that the Big Bastard had put lots of money in it.'

Chris looked puzzled. 'What an odd thing to do.'

I said, 'It's not odd. It's how you buy innocence. You pretend you're paying wages for a service.'

'Well, I wouldn't have thought of it,' he said, and I said, 'Well, I used some of it to buy the knife.'

He clasped his hands together, leaned forward in his chair, and repeated, 'I'm very sorry about what happened to you.'

I thought, 'Oh Chris, you're so sweet. What am I doing to you?'

I said to him, 'Haven't you noticed anything? These last two visits? Something different?'

He looked mystified, and at last I said, 'Come on, Chris! I stopped smoking, because you said you hated it.' I was feeling triumphant.

'You stopped smoking? Just like that? It took me ten years. Congratulations! I'm incredibly impressed . . . and I'm sorry I didn't notice. You must have been dying to tell me.'

'Well,' I said, 'maybe I wasn't as addicted as I thought. Anyway, I could see how much you didn't like it. I got bored with it. You know, I was sitting around too much, drinking all that coffee and getting funny feelings in my chest. I got bored with myself. I got too much of my own company, with all that coffee and smoking. Now I'll just get fat.'

'I'd like you fat, anyway,' said Chris.

When he left for his appointment with Dr Singh, we hugged for a long time on the doorstep, and I could feel all the sympathy coming out of him. I thought what a lovely man he was. I went back inside and sat down by the fire and daydreamed about him.

25
Hostess

Just like everyone else, always waiting for miracles.

I came back just after Wimbledon fortnight. I remember feeling a bit sorry because Chris Evert had just been beaten by Martina Navratilova. It was only because Chris Evert was quite pretty. I wouldn't have cared otherwise. I've known for a long time that I'm quite shallow, but I'm reconciled to it. I get consolation from the thought that everyone probably is.

It was a Monday. You wouldn't think I'd remember that after all these years, but I do, because my daughter had been fiddling again with the settings on the radio in the car, and it was on a pop station, and some man was singing 'Tell me why I don't like Mondays', and I was thinking 'Because everyone hates bloody Mondays, that's why.' I expect that gentlemen of leisure don't like Mondays. Probably even the Queen doesn't.

It was a reasonably good Monday for me, though, because I was going to drop in on Roza, with a big bunch of chrysanthemums.

The Bob Dylan Upstairs opened the door as usual. He had the pretty little blonde with him, and I thought, 'Lucky bastard.' This was the blonde called Sarah who was two-timing the drunken Dutchman, and the Bob

Dylan was actually finding it all very difficult. I still thought 'Lucky bastard', however.

Roza chose this occasion to tell me how she'd got involved in selling herself. I often wonder how people end up doing what they do. How do you become a sweet-shop proprietor, or a tax inspector? How do you become a medical salesman, for that matter? Well, the first thing is that you put your dreams on hold. And the second thing is that you then unintentionally give up your dreams entirely, and you while away your life until death comes to collect you, and then you get that last opportunity to look back and see nothing but emptiness behind you.

Roza put the flowers in a vase, and made some coffee. She said, 'You know, it took me a long time before I slept with anyone again. It's even more complicated when you've been raped lots of times. I got memories that suddenly came back even when I was enjoying it.

'My first man was an oilman from America, called Joe. He was nice. He came to the club just to see me, and he was always good to me. He said his marriage was like the Arizona Desert. The same old story, I heard it so many times. He was lonely and not very happy, and I didn't sleep with him for the money. It was consolation. It wasn't for the sex either. It was just nice to have someone to be close to, and be wrapped up with in bed afterwards. He gave me lots of money, though. He said, "Listen, princess, this isn't payment, it's gratitude, and anyway, I love you. If it wasn't for the kids I'd carry you off anywhere you want to go." Then he got sent to Saudi Arabia, and he gave me a bracelet made of Indian gold, and he said he would come back and see me every time he came through London. He cried the last time I saw him to say goodbye, and then I never saw him again. I think that maybe something must have happened to him, because he wasn't the kind of man to disappear. He was a good man, I could just tell.

'After that, you know, I didn't sleep with any old body. I took the ones I liked. It wasn't like being out in the street, having to go with everyone who stops in a car. You know, I liked it when all these rich men wanted me so much, and a lot of them said, "Let me take you away from all this," just like in the movies, but I didn't want to leave the club. Val and Bergonzi, they were like my mother and father, and it was like my home after a while, and anyway, I never loved any of those men enough to go away with them for good, and by then I needed the champagne. It wasn't like being with Alex, or even Francis and Joe.'

I said, 'But weren't you ever frightened?' and Roza replied, 'I always had the knife in my bag. I would've stuck it in anyone who got rough. It gave me the confidence.'

I looked at Roza smiling at me, and wondered if she really would. At first I almost couldn't imagine her sticking a knife in someone, partisan's daughter or not, but if I thought about it a little longer, it started to seem all too likely.

Roza said, 'You know, in the end, I realised I was corrupted. I was looking at men to see how much money they'd give me, and I wasn't even bothering to think if I liked them any more. Some men, they're very strange, because they get these weird ideas. They want you to piss on them or they want you to beat them, or they want you to dress up like a policewoman, or they want to be treated like a little dog on a lead. My life was getting more and more peculiar, and I had this trunk, and it was just filling up with so much money, I couldn't believe it. It's the trunk under my bed, the black metal one with the red writing on top.'

I said, 'Please stop telling me that. You shouldn't. You shouldn't tell anyone at all.'

'But why shouldn't I tell you?'

I said, 'Because I don't want the temptation. I don't want even the thought of it. You shouldn't be so stupid as to tell anyone whatsoever.'

'I told the Bob Dylan Upstairs,' said Roza, 'but that's all.'

'Well, you shouldn't have,' I said. 'You ought to know better.'

'I didn't buy anything except a television,' said Roza, as if she wanted to change the subject. 'I could buy practically anything, but I just bought a telly, to smoke in front of.'

'Did you sleep with anyone famous?' I asked. I was curious, even though I felt a weight like lead in my stomach. Feeling sick was the price I paid for my curiosity.

'I expect so,' she replied, 'but I didn't know who was famous or not. A lot of men don't tell you who they are. Maybe I had politicians and aristocrats. I don't know. Anyway, you don't remember them after a while. I never had Mick Jagger or Prince Charles. I would have remembered that, maybe. Anyway, all these men had crap wives. I carried on because of the money. I charged more than the other girls. It made me feel good, charging more. I liked the compliments. "You're so beautiful, you're so interesting, you're so intelligent, if I give you ten thousand pounds will you sleep only with me for the next year? I love you, you're such a wonderful lover," and always, "You're so beautiful." It's good to hear those things when you've had maybe too much champagne, and he's got a wallet with five hundred in it, and you're thinking, "Well, why not?"'

'So why did you stop?'

'I'd had enough, that's all. It got so I couldn't remember anything. I was in a very dull dream, where nothing was happening and nothing would ever happen again. You know, the time went by and went by, and it was all just fog. I was going to bed at five in the morning and getting up at five in the evening. If it was winter I never saw the light. I couldn't remember what things looked like. I had to rack my brain to remember a river. I was eating sandwiches and smoking and drinking coffee until it was time to go to Bergonzi's. I only knew it was spring when we had daffodils in the vases. I had another abortion once; there were people who gave me twice as much if I didn't use a johnny, and that gave me some problems, and I had to go off with Val to get it sorted out. After the second abortion I couldn't bear to see a little child. It made me hurt inside, like when someone punches you in the stomach. I know about that because sometimes the alcohol makes men get rough, and it was my job to get them full of champagne.

'I don't know if my life went too fast or too slow. Sometimes it was slow like going to funerals, but the time just disappeared. I didn't have any ideals any more, and I stopped learning anything. I became disappointed in myself.

'Then one day I woke up early, maybe three in the afternoon, and I saw the sunlight shining on the little bits of dust in the air in my room. It was just one ray of light, but it was very beautiful. It made me want to see sunflowers, and the snowstorms you get when the cherry blossom blows off the trees. I thought about Tasha and Fatima, and wondered what they were doing, and my poor father.

'I went and looked in the mirror with the curtain open, just to see what I was, and I looked very hard at that Roza. I was all thin and white like one of those girls at the club who did it for heroin. I touched my face and it was like paper, and I had one or two grey hairs just beginning. I had these thin lines on my mouth and eyes, and they didn't go when I stopped smiling. I remembered how beautiful and healthy I was at the end of the voyage with Francis.

'What I did was, I sat in front of the mirror and I talked to myself. I said, "Roza, you're a stupid bitch," but I didn't say it in an angry way. I said it as if it was a matter of fact. I said, "Hey, Roza, you fucked up the best years of your life." I said, "Your brain's half dead, you stupid bitch." I thought of this excuse, I said, "Yeah, but you were fucked over by the Big Bastard and his shitty friend," and I shrugged, like this, and I replied to myself, "Well, tough shit, Roza. With any luck they're dead. People like that don't get to have long lives." I said to myself, "Hey, Roza, you haven't got any friends except the ones at the club, and you haven't got any dreams, you're just a stupid bitch who crapped on herself."

'I talked with Val and Bergonzi that night, and Bergonzi said, "Well, doll, I wouldn't want to see you go, but enough's enough, innit? This place does you in after a while. Better get out before you ain't got no life left." I said, "I don't really want to go," and Val said, "Well, darlin', it comes sooner or later for all the girls. There's that moment, and they just know they gotta go. We wouldn't take it personal. Between you and me, darlin', we're thinking of selling up and going somewhere nice anyway. There's this little place in Devon we've been thinking about." "Ten years here, and I've got brain damage," said Bergonzi. "You and me both," said Val.

'So I left, and they had a party for me and gave me presents. I cried when I walked out for the last time, and even the Grill gave me a hug. And then a very nice thing happened, because the Bob Dylan Upstairs moved in, and it gave me someone to talk to. I talked and talked until my face nearly fell off. He was building engines up in the top floor because there's no proper roof up there, and he was making big meals in a wok, and he put garlic and onions and tomatoes and oregano in everything, so it reminded me of being in Dalmatia. He got the downstairs toilet working, and he put the doors back on straight, and he found wood in skips and mended the stairs, and he filled up the holes in the walls with white stuff, and he put flowers in tubs out in the backyard, and he cleared away all the chip wrappers from the front. I looked at him and his improvements, and thought, "There's always something to do."

'After we became friends I made him listen to all my poetry.'

'Just as you did with me?'

'Yes, Chris. It was the same. You and the Bob Dylan are the best friends I ever had. You know, I got better because of you and him. He planted sunflowers for me once. He told me all sorts of things about himself. You know, he's always been in love with Françoise Hardy because she reminds him of the first girl he was in love with. He listens to Françoise Hardy when he's not listening to Bob Dylan.'

I couldn't remember who Françoise Hardy was, and once again I had to go and find out later. Apparently Mick Jagger described her as 'the ideal woman'. I suppose there must be such a woman, somewhere. Anyway, it sounded like a good recommendation, and I found a cheap record in WH Smith. I didn't understand the French songs well, but it was all very pleasant and sad. My daughter caught me listening and said it wasn't cool to like Françoise Hardy these days, and I just said, 'Well, I'm not, am I? Dads aren't supposed to be with it, are they?' and she replied scornfully, 'Dad, no one says "with it" any more. And while I'm on the subject, nobody says "square" or "groovy" either.'

I said to Roza, 'I liked listening to your poems, even though I didn't understand a word. It sounded like waves breaking.'

'They're shit,' said Roza, 'I know they are. But all foreign poetry sounds good as long as you don't understand it. Did I ever tell you about the Bob Dylan and the dog?'

'No,' I said, feeling another twinge of jealousy.

'We had this dog next door that was barking and barking and barking, even at night, and we got very annoyed. It was keeping us awake, and you had to keep turning up the television. Anyway, we encouraged each other, and we got more and more angry, and so we went round next door to complain, and we found it was a sick old man who couldn't go out any more, and he had this Alsatian that was just dying of frustration, so we started taking it for walks.

'It was a nice dog, really friendly and silly and bouncy. We threw sticks for it. It smelled very sweet behind the ears, like toast with honey. We took it out at half past five every day, when the Bob Dylan came back from the garage, and in the end the old man just let it out at twenty past five and it came and waited on our doorstep. We took it to the park where there were ducks and little old ladies with bags of bread, and dogs. I got excited about seeing flowers and squirrels again for the first time in years, and I loved those fat bees with their furry backsides sticking out of the bells. If it was sunny we lay on the grass and ate ice cream. When we came home I made Viennese coffee and we carried on talking. In the end the old man died, and the son took the dog, but we still went out in the park.

'You know, going out with the dog was one of the things that brought me back to living. When I leave London I'll miss the little parks with the ducks forever and ever. That's what I love the most.'

I said, 'You're not thinking of going, are you?' The thought made me feel a little desperate, as if I had lost her already.

'I've this idea,' she said. 'I'd like to go back to Zagreb

and finish my degree, and I want to make it up with my father.'

'Don't go,' I said, and she smiled and squeezed my hand. She said, 'You're so sweet.'

I said, 'Do you fancy the Bob Dylan?' and she replied, 'Oh no, it's not him I'd like. He's too young, and he's always sad about something, and he's like a little brother. I want someone more grown up.'

I said, 'Do you still have a disengaged heart?'

'Oh,' she laughed, 'you remembered about Miss Radic.'

I said, 'You're avoiding the question.'

'No. I don't really know. Maybe, maybe not. I don't think I have. I feel better about it all now.'

'Do you think you'd ever do that again?'

'What?'

'You know, sell yourself.'

She looked at me very straight and said, 'No, of course not. But anything's possible, isn't it? Even you might do it if you were desperate. There are men who hang about at public toilets. They're junkies, and they're selling their mouths and backsides, and they're all people who thought they'd never do anything like that.'

'Are there?' I said. 'Really?' and she laughed at me incredulously. 'Maybe I haven't been to the right toilets.' I felt like an innocent.

'Nobody sees what they don't know,' said Roza. 'Maybe it's better like that.' She paused, smiled coyly, and said, 'Next time you come, I've got something I want to tell you.'

'Have you? What is it? Can't you tell me now?'

She raised a teasing eyebrow, and smiled coyly again. 'I'm not telling you now. I've been bursting to tell you for ages, but I didn't have the courage. Now I think I do, so come back in about . . . five days. By the way, I think I've completely run out of stories. I hope it doesn't matter too much. You will come back anyway, won't you?'

I had never seen her more bright-eyed and animated. I left that Monday with the five hundred pounds still nestling in the breast pocket of my jacket, and went to call on Dr Patel, who'd just got excited about a new drug he'd heard about. I said I didn't have a clue when or if it would become available. Doctors are like everyone else, always waiting for miracles.

26

A Malign Part of Myself

You don't have to be mad to long for someone as much as I longed for her.

I was still enduring the sleepless nights and the tormenting desire that didn't even go away when I took direct action or dosed myself up with whisky. Every time I closed my eyes I saw Roza sitting in front of me, talking and smiling. In my imagination she was still smoking, even though she'd given it up. I could see with my mind's eye every curve of her body, and I thought I could imagine perfectly what she looked like when she was naked, especially as I had had glimpses of her in her window, late at night. I could feel her hands and lips on me. I had pretty reveries about marrying her and taking her away and starting a new life with her, full of interest and good conversation, and inexhaustible, languorous sex. I think I was half mad. If I'd been American I probably would have gone to see a psychiatrist. We all get passions, though. You don't have to be mad to long for someone as much as I longed for her. I did what you do; I made her into my entire world, and she became the world in which I lived. I didn't have any plans or hopes that didn't have her in them.

The next time I called in it was the day that Sebastian Coe broke the record for the mile. I'd just heard about it. I remember thinking that there wasn't really much point in running, unless you were being chased. I was glad I wasn't him, doing all that running just for the sake of it. How would it feel to be him as an old man, looking back and realising that he'd spent his entire youth hurtling around running tracks? He could have been learning the piano or something.

Before going to her house I got drunk. It was accidental, in the way that getting drunk often is. I'd gone to the pub at lunchtime with one of my doctors, so I was already primed, and then later on in the evening I'd run into an old friend in Highgate. He was a Cypriot called Alejandro, and we'd been in the school soccer team together. I was the left back and he was the goalkeeper, and he could do the most amazing leaps and dives that were rather more theatrical than effective. I'd seen him from time to time ever since. He had a garrulous wife, five kids, and a job importing all manner of things from Greece and Cyprus, including bouzoukis, pistachio nuts and impoverished relatives. He had a convertible Mercedes, so he took the mickey out of me for having a shit-brown Allegro, and then he persuaded me that we should go out for a meal in a Greek restaurant, so I rang home and said I was going to be late. I could just imagine the Great White Loaf lying in bed snoring when I got back, in a nylon nightie and her hair in curlers, with *She* magazine open at the problem page.

Al had turned into quite a hedonist since I last saw him, and somehow I got caught up in his mood. I don't drink much usually, because it gives me insomnia and tends to make me aggressive, and I hate the feeling of being out of control, but for a while I wasn't too badly affected. I wouldn't normally have had an aperitif, and nor would I have got through that amount of wine, or topped it all off with that Greek brandy. Al was a lot of fun, he knew hundreds of stupid jokes, and being with him was just like being young again. The evening became hilarious, and the Greek waiters made it even worse by giving us a lot of free top-ups, plus plates to smash. Then the patron came and joined us because Al was an old customer, and vaguely related, so the flow of booze became unlimited. I know they were just being hospitable, and I don't blame anyone except myself for what happened afterwards.

Looking back on it, the events that followed had a terrible inevitability about them. I should have taken a taxi home, because I was far too drunk to drive. I turned down Al's offer to sleep at his house, partly because I was frightened of having to explain myself to the Great White Loaf when I finally did get home, and partly because I baulked at the cost of a taxi all the way to Sutton. It was very late, and I thought there wouldn't be much traffic anyway. I did what drunks always do; I underestimated the degree of my drunkenness, and I overestimated my ability to drive.

It is easy enough to drive through Archway if you're going home to Sutton from Highgate. You just go down Highgate Hill. After that I should have gone down Junction Road towards Kentish Town and Camden, but when I got to the big roundabout, I thought, 'Why don't I just drop in on Roza? Yes, I want to see Roza.

I want to see Roza and give her a big hug, and tell her just how wonderful she is.' I remember those words that I was going to say: 'Roza, you really are wonderful.' I went down Holloway Road and turned left into her street. I had only driven a short way, but it was a miracle that I even got that far. I was leaning forwards, staring pop-eyed at the road ahead, and blinking and shaking my head so as not to become hypnotised by it. The wipers were squeaking on the windscreen because it wasn't raining. I think I must have turned them on, thinking that the switch was the one for the lights. That means that I probably didn't have my lights on at all.

When I got to my destination I went and had a long pee in the doorway of one of the boarded-up houses, and I seem to remember not being able to get the zip done up again because my shirt had caught in it. It was a two-handed job to sort the problem out, and I needed one of my hands to hold onto things so that I didn't keel over. My flies must have been undone during everything that ensued. I pressed the bell for quite a long time before I remembered that it had never worked. I banged on the door with my knuckles, and when that didn't work, I started shouting. 'Roza! Roza! It's me! Roza!'

Someone opened a window opposite and a coarse woman's voice said, 'Fuckin' belt up, will you? We're trying to get some bleedin' sleep.' I turned and nearly fell down the steps, but I managed to wave a Harvey Smith at her and say something intelligent like, 'Fuck off, you slag.'

Then Roza opened the door. She was dressed in white pyjamas printed with roses, and a fluffy pink dressing gown with matching fluffy pink slippers. 'Roza!' I said, and lunged at her trying to take her into my arms, but I missed and fell forwards into the hallway, so that she had to step back smartly. I got upright by scrabbling at the wall. I leaned against the doorpost of her room, and looked at her with what I fancied to be doggish devotion. I was sweating, my hair was dishevelled, and my tie at half mast. I discovered in the morning that it had long streaks of congealed taramasalata and hummus down it.

Roza said, 'You're drunk, Chris,' and I said, 'No, I am not, I am not drunk, no, I have never, never, never been more sober in my life.'

She said, 'It's quarter to two in the morning,' and I said, 'Is it? Is it? Really quarter to two? I thought you were used to it.'

'Used to it?'

'In that knocking shop, you know, staying up all night.'

'It was a hostess club,' said Roza.

'It was a knocking shop,' I said, suddenly feeling angry, 'It was a bloody knocking shop. Course it bloody was. What else was it?'

'You're drunk. Just go home, Chris. I'm going back to bed.'

I made an effort to retrieve the situation by being humorous. I went down on one knee and spread my arms, as if pleading. I said, 'Take me with you, Roza, take me to bed with you.'

She looked down at me sternly and said, 'No, Chris, you're drunk. Come back when you're feeling better.'

I felt another surge of rage. In retrospect it's easy to make excuses. I had a lot to be enraged about. I had endured all those years of being taken for granted and being given less and less in return by the parasite at home. I'd been through years of disappointment and self-hatred for never having amounted to anything. I'd seen people all around me apparently living purposeful and happy lives, but all I had managed to achieve was the despair of the common man who lives in a vacuum.

She repeated 'Go home, Chris' and I just exploded. All that bottled-up anger and resentment suddenly welled up out of me. I called her a bitch, among other things. I was reeling about in her hallway, saying, 'Bitch, bitch, you bloody fucking bitch.' Then I heard my own repulsively whiny voice saying, 'Why can't I come to bed with you? Why can't I?'

'After calling me a bitch?'

I swayed on my feet, trying to look her in the eyes, but the effort was too much, so I had to lean back against the wall. I was breathing heavily, and I was just beginning to feel sick. It was then that some malign part of myself made me reach into my breast pocket and take out the Manila envelope full of the crumpled fivers and tenners of the Premium Bond fund that I'd stowed away over the past few months. I waved it in her face contemptuously, and said, 'What about this then? What about this, eh? Does this make any difference? Does it?' I thrust it into her hands.

Roza looked perplexed and said, 'What is it?'

'Five hundred,' I said. 'Five hundred quid. Or has it gone up like every bloody thing else?'

Her face went blank, she looked down at the floor for a very long while, the envelope in her hand, and then she lifted her head and said very softly, 'I always thought you were a very lovely man.' There were tears in her eyes, and they were just beginning to trickle down her cheeks.

That stopped me in my tracks, and my rage abruptly vanished. A great cloud of weariness came down and swallowed me up. I felt so sick at heart that I couldn't say anything at all. I went to the door, paused to get my balance, and then stumbled down the steps.

I drove some way, thinking that I could get home, but then realised that I didn't have a clue where I was. I was also feeling extremely nauseous. I managed to stop the car, and I got out just in time to vomit through the railings of what must have been Clissold Park. I'd been there a few times with Roza when she was on one of her gleeful missions to see old English ladies feeding bread to ducks, and bald deserted middle-aged men throwing sticks into the water for their mongrels.

I was sick for quite a long time. It felt as though I was being kicked in the stomach. I had the horrible acid taste of bile burning in my throat, and thick strings of bitter saliva hanging from my lips. My eyes watered, and my head broke out in a cold perspiration that ran under my shirt collar and down my back.

When it seemed that nothing more would come, I relieved myself through the railings and went back to my car. As I was about to get in I noticed my new tyres, shining in the yellow lamplight, and remembered that I'd bought them with money from the envelope. The thought of her counting it made me wince. I started up the Allegro and got as far as the end of Clissold Road before I realised that there was not the slightest chance of my ever getting home. I ran the car up against the kerb and turned off the ignition. I managed to clamber into the back of the car, wrapped the rug around me and fell into a stupor.

I woke up in the morning, stiff and aching as if I had been run over, just when everyone was going to work. I sat up in the back, and was astonished to see the Bob Dylan Upstairs walking past in overalls, carrying his blue box of tools. I realised after a few moments that I'd parked right outside the scruffy little Morris Minor garage where he was working.

I didn't want him to see me, so when he'd gone in, I hurriedly got out of the back, and into the front. I drove as far the Wington Green roundabout, and on a strange impulse turned off into Mildmay Road. There I parked up in a resident's space, dropped my forehead onto the steering wheel, and wept.

27
Holes in my Guts

When the Bob Dylan Upstairs answered the door, he said, 'You'd better come in.'

I had left it a week. I knew perfectly well that I should have come back immediately to apologise, but such was my humiliation and mortification, and such was my shame, that I just couldn't bear to face her. Now I'd come at last, cringing inside, my hands trembling, my cheeks burning with embarrassment. In my arms I bore a huge and overpoweringly fragrant bunch of fifty red roses.

I went inside and apprehended it all as if with new eyes, the wires hanging off the walls, the crude dusty bathroom with no plaster on the laths, the creaking carpetless staircase down into the basement, the weird swirling graffiti left by former occupants.

I said, 'Where's Roza?'

'I don't know,' replied the Bob Dylan. 'She's gone.'

'Gone?'

'She left at the weekend. This big van turns up, and she and this tall man just load it up and leave. I haven't a clue where's she's gone. What I do know is that she just sat in her room crying.'

'Crying?'

'She wouldn't open the door. I brought her tea and

things, but I had to leave them outside the door. The sobbing was very hard to listen to, I can tell you. I don't know what you did to her, but anyway, now she's left, and she was still crying when she went.'

'I didn't do anything to her,' I protested.

'Obviously you did. The one thing she told me was that you'd come round drunk in the middle of the night and been vile to her.' He looked at me very coldly, and added, 'She was very fond of you. She often told me.'

'Did she leave a forwarding address? Anywhere I can write to?'

'No. Some things arrived in the post and I don't know what to do with them.' He gestured towards a small heap of letters on the floor of the hallway. I picked them up and looked through them. I was puzzled. I said, 'This one's for Dubrovka, and this one's for Josipa, and this one's for Sacha.'

'Well, they're all Roza. There's one for Marija as well.'

'Why so many different names?'

'Well, do you know who she really was?'

'What do you mean, "who she really was"?'

The Bob Dylan looked at me wryly, and said, 'Well, I never assumed that I knew exactly who she was. She was Sharon Didsbury for the purposes of the rent book. As you know, I'm supposed to be someone called John Horrocks. And the sculptress who's supposed to be upstairs and no one ever sees is supposed to be Ruthie, but her real name's Amanda. This is a whole house full of people who are up to something. All I know about Roza is what she told me.'

'Did she tell you the same things as she told me?'

'Well, how would I know?'

'Did she tell you about sleeping with her father, and the black trunk under her bed, full of money?'

'Oh yes, she told me about that. I never looked inside it to check, though.'

'Did she tell you about being abducted?'

'To the special raping house? Yes, she told me that one as well. Did she tell you about murdering one of the men who did it?'

I shook my head. 'She told me she bought a knife to do it with, but she never saw him again. She never said she'd killed him.'

The Bob Dylan laughed. 'Well, she told me that he eventually came back to the club, and she got him very drunk and took him in a taxi to a disused warehouse in the docks, that she'd already reconnoitred, and she stuck the knife in him just when he thought she was going to give him a blow job. That was how she got the correct angle to get it under the ribs. She was very keen on getting the right angle. She mentioned it quite a lot. It was something her father told her about, apparently.'

I was stunned. 'She told you that? Maybe she didn't want to shock me. Maybe that's why she didn't tell me. She showed me a knife.'

'That was a very sharp knife.'

'Didn't you think that you ought to go to the police?'

'Only for a second. I looked into myself and couldn't feel sorry for him, if that's what really happened.'

It suddenly occurred to me to doubt everything she had told me, and the implications of that doubt began to carve holes in my guts. I didn't know what to do or say. The Bob Dylan said, 'You can't know anything about anyone in this house except what you get told. I could tell you I was the illegitimate son of the Shah of Iran, and you wouldn't know whether I was or not, would you?'

'But why would you tell me that?'

The Bob Dylan looked at me pityingly, and said, 'You might be a whole lot older than me, but you have a few gaps, haven't you? People tell stories to make themselves more interesting. Sometimes they do things just so they can tell the story afterwards. I've done that myself. If Roza kept you intrigued it was because she wanted you to keep coming back. I sometimes thought that she told them all to me as a dress rehearsal for telling them to you. Maybe you can work out for yourself why she did that.'

'I've never talked to you properly before, have I?' I said.

'I've got some stories,' he answered, 'but you probably wouldn't fancy me enough to want to hear them.'

'I was just thinking,' I said, 'that it's a pity that I can't really introduce you to my daughter. She loves Bob Dylan, for one thing. You'd be a boyfriend I could put up with. I could introduce you if you promise not to tell her that I ever came here.'

He smiled and said, 'I'll take that as a compliment, but honestly I've got plenty to worry about without your daughter. It's hard enough coping with Sarah.' He handed one of the letters on the floor to me. It was the brown Manila envelope with the five hundred pounds in it. She'd written '*Chris*' on the front.

Inside with the money was a note written neatly in blue ballpoint on the kind of pink paper covered in tiny squares that you use for mathematics. It just said, '*Mislila sam da me volis.*'

I showed it to the Bob Dylan, and he shrugged and said, 'It must be Serbo-Croat.' I said, 'Don't the Serbs use the same letters as the Russians, though? This is in normal letters.'

'I think the Croats use Roman script,' he said.

'She used to say how much she hated Croats.'

'Well, sometimes I hate the English. I am one, though. Anyway, any educated Serb would know how to use Roman letters, wouldn't they?'

I went back there many times to ask the Bob Dylan if there had been sight or sound of Roza, but there was never any news. Her pile of letters got larger and larger. I wish now that I'd taken some of them away and read them, or got them translated. I didn't, out of belated respect. Then finally I went back one day and the Bob Dylan had gone as well. I have no idea where he went or what happened to him. I don't even know his real name, just that he was pretending to be someone called John Horrocks for the purposes of the rent book, and sometimes wore his predecessor's huge moccasins.

So many years went by, with me looking futilely for Roza, making enquiries, writing to embassies and even to Zagreb University. I easily spent a lot more than the five hundred pounds in searching. Half a dozen times I took my wife to Yugoslavia just to poke around, and she just thought we were having strange holidays. I got to know a very great deal about the place, and after a while I started to feel like an honorary Yugoslav. I felt a deep pang when Tito died, and wondered how Roza must be feeling. Eight years later I was thinking of her again when

Albanians started attacking Serbs in Kosovo, and everything over there began to fall apart like a house of cards. I worried in case she had got caught up in all the furore, or dived into the great national depression afterwards, as Serbia became the world's fastest-shrinking country. I wondered if she remembered me with any affection.

As for me, I always thought of her as my one great last chance. After Roza I never had the heart to try again.

Of course, I went and got her note translated immediately, but I have pondered for years the meaning and ramifications of the message that she had written in Serbo-Croat just so that I would have to go to some trouble to find out what it meant. I went to the Yugoslav Embassy at 28 Belgrave Square, and the woman at reception translated it for me, raising her eyebrows archly as she handed the paper back to me, and commenting, 'Well, that's very sad and pathetic.'

I am an old man now, and that tongue of flame leapt up a long time ago, but I have never lost the pain in the chest and the ache in my throat that Roza left behind. I've lived with it, without it ever getting any smaller or less painful. It's been like a metaphysical cancer. Never for a moment have I forgotten her soft sweet voice as she told me all her stories, but sometimes it's hard to remember what she looked like, because I never even had a photograph. The sorry thing is that if we passed in the street nowadays, we probably wouldn't even recognise each other. I do look at everyone, but I've stopped looking with any expectation. I may have stopped searching, but I haven't given up hope. Sometimes, just when I think I've stopped at last, the hope surprises me by coming back.

I know approximately how much time I have left. My hands are becoming a little more weak every day now, and it is possible to calculate the rate at which the disease spreads.

As I said, my wife's dead. I do think about her a great deal, and I surprise myself sometimes by how much I miss her. I loved her very much to begin with, for the first four years or so, but then I came to resent her very angrily and bitterly. In the end I mainly felt sorry for her, because she had just existed from day to day, had never really done her best, lived her whole life without passions, and didn't understand why anyone else might have any.

I can't work out why she chose me in the first place. What was she thinking? That anyone would do? Why did she take it as a matter of course that she was entitled to appropriate my life, and waste it? Did she never feel the slightest twinge of regret on my behalf? She should have found someone more like herself, instead of leading me by the nose into the dismal unlit tunnel of her superfluous life.

I'd love to pass the last days of my life with my daughter. She's a fireball, completely unlike her mother, and she's the one great thing that I've contributed to the world, but she's in New Zealand, and the last thing I'd want is to be a burden to her when she's just becoming successful and making a name for herself. New Zealand is a lovely place. It's just like England was when I was young, full of quiet, decent, humorous people who eat bread and butter and whose clothes don't quite fit. She's on her second marriage now, and I've only met the new man once.

I'm thinking of selling the house in Sutton, so that I can afford the care I'm just about to need. These days I can't hear very well, either, and when you can't hear properly you get very isolated. You find yourself pretending to understand what people are saying, when really you don't. You are never sure what's going on, and it can be very tiresome for other people, having to shout at you or write things down.

I have happy memories of things that happened a long time ago, at the childhood house in Shropshire, with my brother and sisters, or when Roza was telling me her stories in front of the gas fire in that derelict building.

I'm still the kind of man who doesn't go to prostitutes and, as it turned out, I never did resort to one in all my life.

The Bob Dylan Upstairs must be in his fifties. I wonder if he ever made anything of himself. I thought he probably would. I doubt he turned out quite as unconventional as he might have wished, but he was bright, and people like that get to the summit by unexpected routes, in my experience. I wonder if he's still playing 'Für Elise' on the electric guitar. I wonder if he's still got the giant moccasins.

I kept Roza's last message to me. The paper became very dirty and flimsy from being kept in my wallet, and it began to tear along the folds. I put tape on it to keep it together, and when eventually the tape went yellow and inflexible, I went to the library and had it laminated. Now that everyone's gone, and I'm living by myself, I have it stuck on the wall above my desk with Blu-Tack. From time to time I put on my glasses and look at the looped Continental handwriting across the pink squares of that mathematical paper. I try to imagine her face, and her mouth saying just those words. I think I can see the reproachful expression in her eyes, and feel the stab of pain that she must have felt. After Roza I lived my life with a deep sense of shame that I have never been able to shake off.

I think about my last meeting with her, about how she never had the opportunity to say whatever it was that she'd been working herself up to telling me, about how she cried for days afterwards, and then packed up and ran away. The more I think about it the more I think it can only have meant one thing. It's the only way to make sense of what she wrote.

The message was: 'I thought you loved me.'